Dylan cocked his head. "Listen."

Amid the waves crashing on the rocks came the tinny sound of a ringing phone. He took two steps closer to the low metal barrier around the edge of the overlook. "Dial again."

With a shaky finger Mia punched the button to redial. The phone rang again, the ocean breeze snatching the sound so that it seemed to surround her.

Dylan dropped to his knees, skimming the light from his flashlight along the ledge of rock. "It's there, just below the ledge."

He flattened to his belly and army-crawled toward the edge.

The knots that had been forming in Mia's stomach the minute she heard the disembodied phone ringing cinched tighter. "Be careful."

Dylan scooted forward another few inches and then swore.

Clutching her sweater around her trembling body, Mia shuffled to the edge of the precipice. "What is it, Dylan?"

Her gaze followed the beam of his light as it tripped down the vicious rocks. White foam rushed in and swirled around the rocks and something else...a body.

CAROL ERICSON

DECEPTION

HARLEQUIN®
entertain, enrich, inspire™

For LAPD Detective Pete Wilson,
who always gets the bad guys.

Recycling programs
for this product may
not exist in your area.

ISBN-13: 978-0-373-74700-9

DECEPTION

Copyright © 2012 by Carol Ericson

All rights reserved. Except for use in any review, the reproduction or utilization of this work in whole or in part in any form by any electronic, mechanical or other means, now known or hereafter invented, including xerography, photocopying and recording, or in any information storage or retrieval system, is forbidden without the written permission of the publisher, Harlequin Enterprises Limited, 225 Duncan Mill Road, Don Mills, Ontario M3B 3K9, Canada.

This is a work of fiction. Names, characters, places and incidents are either the product of the author's imagination or are used fictitiously, and any resemblance to actual persons, living or dead, business establishments, events or locales is entirely coincidental.

This edition published by arrangement with Harlequin Books S.A.

For questions and comments about the quality of this book please contact us at CustomerService@Harlequin.com.

® and TM are trademarks of Harlequin Enterprises Limited or its corporate affiliates. Trademarks indicated with ® are registered in the United States Patent and Trademark Office, the Canadian Trade Marks Office and in other countries.

www.Harlequin.com

Printed in U.S.A.

ABOUT THE AUTHOR

Carol Ericson lives with her husband and two sons in Southern California, home of state-of-the-art cosmetic surgery, wild freeway chases, palm trees bending in the Santa Ana winds and a million amazing stories. These stories, along with hordes of virile men and feisty women, clamor for release from Carol's head. It makes for some interesting headaches until she sets them free to fulfill their destinies and her readers' fantasies. To find out more about Carol, her books and her strange headaches, please visit her website, www.carolericson.com, "where romance flirts with danger."

Books by Carol Ericson

HARLEQUIN INTRIGUE

*Brothers in Arms
**Guardians of Coral Cove

CAST OF CHARACTERS

Dylan Reese—Coral Cove's new police chief, he swore he'd never walk in his father's shoes. But a botched undercover assignment has driven him back to his hometown and into the orbit of the one woman he could never forget…who now needs his protection more than ever.

Mia St. Regis—The owner of Columbella House, she played a practical joke on her twin sister, Marissa, that she's regretted ever since. Now, with the help of Dylan Reese, the man who'd always had her back, she wants to set things right with both her sister and Columbella House. But someone is determined to see her fail at both.

Marissa St. Regis—Mia's twin sister, she took off for parts unknown when Mia tricked her out of Columbella House. Is she still holding a grudge or is her continued absence a sign of something more sinister?

Peter Casellas—Mia's soon-to-be ex-husband was fine with the terms of their sham marriage, but now he's in financial trouble and he wants Mia to pay…and pay big.

Kayla Rutherford—The result of Marissa St. Regis's secret teen pregnancy, Kayla wants what's rightfully hers, even if she has to take it.

Tyler Davis—The mayor of Coral Cove always wants what's best for his small town, and he'll do anything to protect its image.

Linda Davis—The mayor's wife has a vested interest in Mia's decision about Columbella House, but is her interest purely civic-minded or does it hint at some deeper secret?

Charlie Vega—This local contractor with money problems hits the jackpot when he discovers he's the father of a St. Regis, and he wants his slice of the action.

Tina Vega—Charlie's wife is not happy to discover her husband has an illegitimate daughter with Marissa St. Regis. Will she take out her anger on her husband or his daughter?

Chapter One

Your sister is dead. The words on the screen blurred together, and Mia St. Regis slammed down the cover of the laptop to dismiss them. Why should she take the word of a ditzy psychic like Kylie Grant?

Mia stretched her arms over her head, and then slumped against the soft cushions on the love seat in the corner of the coffeehouse. Of course, here she sat in Coral Cove, but it hadn't been Kylie's email that had prompted her return.

She had to do something with the old ancestral home, Columbella House, before it fell into the sea. Maybe she should just let it.

She swept her computer from the low table in front of her and shoved it into her bag. Shaking back her sleeve, she glanced at her watch. She still had time to check out the family manse before it got completely dark. She'd have to make arrangements to turn on the electricity and whatever else needed connecting out there.

"Bye, thanks." As she pushed off the love seat, she waved to the barista clearing stale breakfast goodies from the glass-enclosed shelves.

The young woman peered over the top of the glass case. "Are you really going to turn Columbella House into some kind of resort?"

Mia banged her shin against the table. "Huh?"

"You're Mia St. Regis, right?"

"Uh, yeah." This girl had probably been in grade school the last time Mia graced the shores of Coral Cove. How the hell did she know her identity?

"The article in the *Coral Cove Herald* said you were coming home to turn Columbella into a beach resort. Cool."

Mia hitched her bag over her shoulder and strode toward the counter. She must've looked as ornery as she felt because the young woman dropped to her heels and took a step back.

"There was an article about me in that little paper?"

The barista bit her lip and pointed an unsteady finger with black polish on the nail toward the front door of the coffeehouse. "The papers are still in the rack if you want to read the article."

Mia spun around and zeroed in on a wire rack near the door sporting a few throwaway papers and the *Coral Cove Herald*. "Definitely want to read that."

"Okay, well, have a nice night." The young woman had backed up a few more steps and crossed her arms.

Mia's heels clipped across the wood floor, and then she paused by the rack and slid a paper off the top of the stack. Her jaw tightened as she took in the picture of her smiling face next to an article with the headline Columbella Heiress Has Remodeling Plans.

With narrowed eyes, she squinted at the byline—Jimmy Holt. She knew that name: some journalism dweeb from high school. So much for flying in here under the radar.

Another face on the front page caught her attention—windswept hair, high, broad cheekbones, strong chin, intense stare—Dylan Reese. She scanned that headline, too—Another Chief Reese.

So Dylan had filled his father's shoes as police chief of Coral Cove. The single ladies in town must be licking their chops over that news. In fact, she had to wipe a little drool from the corner of her own mouth. Even though Dylan had always treated her as an annoying sister, his general gorgeousness hadn't escaped her.

She stuffed the paper in the side pocket of her laptop case and swung out the door. She'd had a long flight from New York to San Francisco that morning, and a long drive from the city down the coast to Coral Cove. But the coffee had fortified her and she wanted a look at the old place before the darkness descended. She even had a flashlight for the occasion.

Standing by the alley entrance where she'd parked her rental, she closed her eyes and let the cool air brush her skin. Summer nights in Coral Cove never got too warm. The humidity never got too high. She filled her lungs with the salty air and exhaled slowly.

Okay, maybe she did miss a few things about her hometown.

"Chief, Chief. Someone's in my parking space."

Mia's eyes flew open and she spun around. One of the merchants on Main Street had snagged the new chief and was dragging him to his private parking space...where she'd stashed her rental car.

She strode into the alley and beeped the remote. "That's my car."

The chief, Dylan Reese, turned a pair of dark blue eyes on her and the temperature in Coral Cove, along with the humidity, shot up a few degrees.

"That's my private space. You can't park there." The merchant waved his arms around while hopping up and down next to the chief, like a bird on hot cement.

Or maybe he just seemed so agitated because Chief Reese had a silent, still presence, like he was sizing up the situation and deciding which one of them to shoot first.

Mia slid between the two men, yanked open the

back door and dropped her laptop case on the seat. "Sorry. I didn't realize Main Street had reserved parking spots."

The little man jabbed at a metal sign over the space that read Reserved for Owner.

"Oops, my bad."

"Give her a ticket, Chief. She's in violation."

"She might be in violation...of a lot of things, but she's moving the car now, Leon."

Leon shook a stubby finger at her. "You may own the biggest house in town, that eyesore on the coast, but you don't own Main Street."

Who *didn't* know her identity?

Mia raised one brow. "Not yet."

That sent Leon sputtering and muttering back to the side entrance of his antiques store.

"Making friends and influencing people already, Mia?"

She laughed and stuck out her hand. "As usual. How are you, Dylan, or should I call you Chief?"

"Dylan or Chief is a lot better than some of the names you used to call me." He took her hand, engulfing it in a warm, rough clasp, and pulled her in for a peck on the cheek.

A brotherly peck on the cheek.

Her gaze dropped from his handsome face, a little thinner, a little craggier than she'd remembered, and then flitted across his broad chest as it stretched the khaki material of his uniform. He looked about as good in that uniform as he'd look out of it.

He squeezed her hand harder, as if he knew her mind had wandered into dangerous territory. As she slipped her hand from his, she noticed the tail end of a tattoo peeking out of his long sleeve. Had the chief taken a trip on the wild side before settling into law enforcement like his father?

She laughed again, this time to cover the confusion she felt at his touch. Dylan always had the looks, but Mia had been friends with his twin sister, Devon, and had always valued him as a brother. She'd always wished *her* twin had been a brother.

Your sister is dead.

A sliver of anxiety needled her flesh, and the laugh died on her lips.

"Are you okay? I'm not going to give you a ticket for parking in Leon's special space."

And just like the Dylan of old, he could tune in to her feelings. "I'm fine. Lot of ghosts in this town."

"If a ghost…or anyone else…starts getting to you, give me a holler."

"Thanks, Chief. See you around." She scanned the sky, streaked with orange and red. She'd need that flashlight for Columbella after all.

Dylan stood with his hands shoved into his pockets, one shoulder leaning against the brick façade of Leon's store, watching her as she slipped into the car.

She cranked on the engine and waved. Why

would anyone else in town get to her? Dylan's words had carried an edge of warning, or the town was already casting its spell on her.

Cruising down Main Street, she glanced right and left at the new shops and restaurants. She'd picked late August to take care of business to avoid the height of the summer tourist season.

She'd also avoided quite a bit of drama over the summer, most of it occurring at Columbella House, which had given her further incentive to take some action. She hadn't needed Kylie-the-fortune-teller's email about her sister to make a journey to Coral Cove.

She pointed her car toward the Coast Highway, but turned right toward Columbella instead of left toward her motel. She'd lingered in the coffeehouse and on the sidewalk chatting to Dylan a little too long, and now the sun had dipped halfway into the ocean. But meeting up with Dylan had been worth it.

Chewing her lip, she squinted into the headlights of an oncoming car. She should've called the electric company from New York so she wouldn't have to stumble around with a flashlight in the house. Maybe it would be better to view the house and assess the damages in the light of day…when the ghosts were sleeping.

She pinned her shoulders against the car seat. No time like the present. She'd take a quick peek and then return tomorrow.

She'd put off dealing with the *eyesore,* as that shopkeeper had called it, for several years. Might as well dive right in.

She took the turnoff to Coral Cove Drive and rolled down the darkened street. Since Columbella took up a huge portion of the street and no light came from the house, it cast most of the block in darkness, giving it an eerie vibe.

The Roarkes lived in Hawaii now, visiting only sporadically. A light glowed on the porch of the Girard house. Michelle had stayed on in the house after her father died. Michelle was a teacher, so maybe she was still enjoying the last few weeks of summer before school started. Lights also dotted the Vincents' place— looked like they might be home.

Mia blew out a breath—not as deserted as she'd feared, not that she feared Columbella House. After all, most of the wacky people who had done wacky things in this house were *her* wacky people.

She pulled into the long driveway and cut the engine. The house had been built into the rock and a portion of it hung over the ocean. Her great-grandfather had harbored some strange notions of what an appropriate beach house should entail. Stepping out of the car, she soaked in the sound of the waves crashing below, and she could almost feel the salty sea spray on her face.

She'd put the key to the house on her key chain, which she swung around her finger as she walked up the steps. She stumbled on a portion of the crumbled porch and flicked on her flashlight, sweeping the beam of light across the entrance. Mia hunched her shoulders. Old Leon had hit the nail on the head—*eyesore*.

The key scraped as she shoved it into the rusty lock, the sound sending a chill zigzagging down her spine. *Don't be ridiculous.* She pushed open the door and straightened that same spine, banishing the chill.

She was a St. Regis. This house belonged to her. Even the ghosts belonged to her, and she was ready to take names and kick some spirit heinie.

Stepping into the entrance hall, she bathed the walls and ceiling with the beam of her flashlight. A chandelier tinkled above her—dusty, but still a beautiful antique. The staircase twisted in front of her, and she scanned the two landings for signs of any more hanging bodies. Apparently, Columbella House had become the *de rigueur* place to commit suicide.

She trailed her hand along the wall and turned the corner into the sitting room. A couple of men had been killed in here a few months ago. Kieran Roarke had saved Dylan's sister's little boy. Where had Dylan been on that one?

Sheets covered most of the furniture. Some had slipped off here and there, and dust blanketed the exposed pieces. Wouldn't Leon love to get his pudgy hands on this stuff?

Mia wandered into the library, and her light played over the scorched wall, a grim reminder of another death in the house. She'd known about the secret room off the library, but the house hadn't given up all its secrets to her...or anyone.

Creeping into the hidden room, she clutched her purse to her chest. A serial killer had died in this room, one of her second cousins once or twice removed. Not removed enough. Why did this house attract all the kooks and weirdos?

A board creaked on the stairs and she spun around, dropping her flashlight. The flashlight rolled, throwing distorted shadows on the walls. Mia gulped in a few breaths and lunged for the flashlight. She scooped it up and charged into the library.

Hadn't that sheet been covering the chair in the corner when she'd walked in here? Had that mirror been cracked?

She sped out of the library, keeping the line of light in front of her, looking neither left nor right. She glanced over her shoulder once at the spiral staircase. Something was hanging from the third-floor landing, but she had no intention of investigating.

She blew out the front door and slammed it behind her. Then she raced to her rental car and locked all the doors. Breathing heavily, she gripped the steering wheel with both hands.

Then she laughed. She'd allowed the old place to

get to her, even though she'd sworn she wouldn't. She started the car and backed out of the driveway. What kind of lunatic visited a haunted house at night on her own, anyway? The seeds of madness in the St. Regis family must've sprouted in her head, too.

She careened back onto the highway and accelerated, buzzing down the window so she could breathe and think. She'd head back tomorrow and assess the condition of the house. Maybe she'd clean up a bit, and then talk to a couple of Realtors in town, starting with the mayor's wife, Linda Davis. Mia might restore the old place to its former grandeur, or she'd demo the whole thing and start over with a modern hotel.

The car picked up speed downhill, and she pumped the brakes a few times as she hugged the curve in the road. This little rental jobby sure didn't perform like her Lexus. She squeezed the brake pedal again, and the car barely responded. Her tires squealed as they gripped for purchase on the road, churning up gravel from the shoulder on her right, which descended to the rocky cliffs above the ocean.

As she came out of the turn, the car zoomed forward, and she jammed her foot on the brake. The car lurched and shuddered, and she gripped the steering wheel with clammy hands. It didn't want to stop.

A turnout for a viewpoint loomed ahead, its steel

guardrail acting as a barrier to the cliffs. Mia eased the wheel to the right, glancing in her rearview mirror. A car coming the other direction honked. She aimed the car toward the turnout, and it jostled as it left the smooth asphalt. Mia stomped on the parking brake and the car skidded into the wide turnout.

Her back wheels fishtailed, sending the car into a spin. The right side of the car slammed into the guardrail. The air bag exploded, pinning her against the seat and knocking the wind out of her. Mia gritted her teeth against the scraping, tearing noise of metal on metal. A shower of sparks flashed outside the passenger window.

The car heaved to a stop, but she could still hear something spinning. Her nostrils flared at the smell of burning rubber.

She pushed against the air bag, and the car tilted to the side. Turning her head, she rested her cheek against the air bag and peered out the passenger window. Her heart slammed against her rib cage and she managed a small whimper.

The right side of her car was hanging over the edge, and she was looking at a sheer drop onto some vicious rocks before they tumbled into the ocean.

One more inch and she'd be getting the view of her life…the last view of her life.

Chapter Two

As he strode toward the mangled car, Dylan swore, the adrenaline pumping the words to his lips. One side of the car that had just been parked illegally in Leon's spot, Mia's rental car, now hung precariously over a cliff. His gaze scanned the ground— no body. So that meant Mia was still in the car... over the edge.

The radio in his car crackled—a 911 emergency call to this very spot. Someone else must've seen the crash.

"Mia?" He edged closer to the car and the open window, not wanting to upset its precarious balancing act.

"Dylan?" Her word came out on a sob.

"It's going to be fine. Don't move."

"It's going to go over, isn't it? The car's going over."

Not if I can help it. "No. I'll get you out of there before that happens."

"I'm afraid to move. The air bag has me pinned down, and I don't want to struggle against it."

"Good idea." He hovered over the car and lifted the door handle. "Can you unlock the door?"

"I—I think so."

He heard a click and let out a pent-up breath.

"Someone must've seen you go over. Emergency vehicles are on the way." The car rocked and a tumble of rocks slid down the side of the cliff.

But would they get here in time?

Dylan eased open the car door. The car tilted back toward him. That was a good sign.

"Unlatch your seat belt, very carefully."

She shifted against the air bag, and the click from the seat belt sounded like a shot.

"You're halfway there, Mia." He shuffled closer to the car, holding his breath as if a puff could send the car hurtling over the cliff.

He tensed his muscles and slid an arm between Mia's back and the car seat. He curled it around her waist. "Okay, I'm going to pull you out all at once. Don't hesitate to come to me."

Dylan braced his foot against the car and pulled Mia toward him, dislodging her from her position wedged behind the air bag.

He staggered backward, dragging her along, until he stumbled and fell to the ground.

Her soft body landed on top of him.

Then a creak ripped through the air and they both looked up in time to see the rental car slide down the cliff. Several seconds later, a crash shook the ground.

A ripple rolled through Mia's body and Dylan clutched her closer. "It's okay. I got you."

Sirens wailed in the distance while black smoke rose from the explosion on the rocks. The smell of gasoline overpowered the salty air.

Mia drew in short puffs of air against his chest, sucking in his khaki shirt with each breath. His hands lingered over her hair and he wanted to smooth his palms over the silky strands, but it felt like taking advantage of her vulnerable condition.

A fire truck wheeled into the turnout, and Mia jerked up her head. Her glassy eyes reflected the revolving red lights. The wail that assaulted their ears seemed to jolt her out of her shock.

She sat upright, straddling Dylan's hips. He didn't mind, but she quickly took stock of her position and rolled from his body, staggering to her bare feet. Her shoes must've fallen off in the car.

He jumped up next to her. "Are you okay? Did you lose control of the car?"

Shaking her head, she bent over and brushed the dirt and gravel from her flowery skirt. The toes of her bare feet curled into the gritty ground. "The brakes went out on me."

The firefighters scrambled from the truck and rushed to the edge of the overlook. Then the fire captain, Dave Melendez, peeled away and approached them. He nodded at Dylan. "Hey, Chief. Miss, is that your car?"

"That *was* my car, or rather the rental company's car."

"Are you all right?"

"I'm okay. Shaken up." She waved a hand in Dylan's direction. "Dyl…Chief Reese came to my rescue."

The ambulance roared into the overlook and squealed to a stop. Dylan held up both hands to slow them down. Thank God the EMTs wouldn't be scraping anyone off those rocks down there.

Melendez asked, "Did you see what happened, Chief?"

"No, just the aftereffects. Ms. St. Regis's car had plowed through the guardrail and was hanging halfway over the cliff with her in it."

The captain whistled. "You're lucky you got out of there before it went over."

"Thanks to the chief." Mia rubbed her arms. "He pulled me out before it went kaplooey."

Dylan shrugged out of his windbreaker and draped it over Mia's shoulders. His arm followed, as she swayed forward and he clamped her body to his.

An EMT, Patrick O'Shea, charged into the group. Dylan knew him, too—one of the more interesting aspects of working in a small town.

"Sit down, Ms. St. Regis. We'll check you out."

Mia wrinkled her nose, probably wondering how everyone in town knew her name. "I'm fine. Just a little unsteady."

"You have an abrasion on your chin. Did the air bag deploy?"

Mia touched her fingertips to her reddened chin. "Yes."

"You'll probably have some bruising on your arms, too." O'Shea jerked his thumb toward the back of the ambulance. "Have a seat and we'll check out your vitals."

She took a few shuffling steps away from Dylan, and he placed his hands on her shoulders to guide her to the ambulance. He exerted a little pressure to get her to sit in the back of the ambulance since she still seemed incapable of voluntary movement.

Melendez had returned from his investigation at the edge of the lookout. "They put out the fire. Not much damage from that, but the car's pretty smashed up."

Mia struggled against the blood pressure cuff secured around her arm. "My purse! My laptop! My...shoes."

"Don't worry about that now, Ms. St. Regis. We'll salvage what we can, right, Chief?"

"But my laptop. I have...stuff on there."

Dylan squeezed her knee. "Once they bring up the wreckage, I'll have a few of my guys sort through it. Not sure your laptop would survive that drop and then the explosion that followed. I hope you have a backup for all those fancy designs you create."

"Fancy...?" She settled back on the ambulance

and let the EMT finish his inventory of her vitals. "Oh, you mean my work."

What did *she* mean? Did she have photos of her family on there—husband, children? He'd never bothered to ask…too busy drinking in the sight of her with her gleaming chestnut hair and big brown eyes. She had the looks to be a model herself, but not the height. She barely reached his shoulder.

"Are you about finished with the patient?" Dylan wedged his boot against the tire of the ambulance. "She needs a ride home and a good, hot meal."

O'Shea looked up from shining a light in Mia's eyes. "Taking this chief stuff seriously, huh, Reese?"

"I run a full-service department. You ready, Mia?"

Her eyes widened, the dilated pupils making them look even darker. "You're going to take me back to my motel?"

"Sure. I guess your exploration of the old homestead is going to have to wait until tomorrow."

"I…I guess so."

Dylan scratched his chin. "We'll haul the car to Ted's Garage. Maybe he can figure out what went wrong. The rental car company's going to demand that anyway. They'll probably try to put the blame on you."

She pushed off the back of the ambulance, steadier on her feet this time. "Let 'em try. I wasn't even speeding. I started going downhill, pumped the brakes a bit and…nada…they wouldn't work."

"You were going *downhill?*" Coming from town, he thought, she should've been going uphill. "I'm glad I was on the road tonight."

"Me, too." She dipped her head and scooted off the edge of the ambulance. "Did you call 911, too?"

"No. That call had already gone in by the time I saw your car." He waved to the fire captain. "Hey, Dave. Do you know who made the 911 call?"

"I don't know. You'll have to check with dispatch." He tilted his head toward the clutch of firemen peering over the edge of the cliff, now joined by four cops in uniform—Dylan's entire on-duty squad. "Your boys are calling in for a truck and a crane. My guys will make their way down there and try to get that hunk of junk up top."

Mia hugged herself and hunched her shoulders. "I could've been part of that junk."

"But you're not." Dylan snaked an arm around her again, his fingers tangling in her hair.

Her lips twitched into a smile, but her brow furrowed. "Don't worry about dinner. All my money and credit cards are probably floating in the ocean about now."

"No problem. You can pay me back."

"Just like the brother I never had—but really, I'm not hungry." She slugged him in the shoulder, and he winced—not because she packed a powerful punch, but the reference to being a brother had just cut him off at the knees.

He gave her a little shove from behind toward his squad car. "Wait for me in the car…and watch where you're walking with those bare feet."

After consulting with the accident scene investigators and his officers, Dylan slid into the car and eyed Mia slumped in his backseat. "You could've sat up front, you know, so you don't look like a suspect."

Sitting up, she curled her fingertips into the wire mesh that separated the front seat from the back. "Wasn't sure I was allowed next to all those gadgets."

"I trust you." He wheeled his squad car to the edge of the turnout. "Where are you staying?"

"I'm at the Sea View Motel."

As he pulled onto the highway, Dylan knitted his brows. "That's in the other direction. What were you doing on this stretch of the highway?"

"I went to the house."

"Columbella House?"

"Is there any other?"

"It's dark." He adjusted his mirror. "What did you hope to find there?"

She flopped back against the seat again. "I don't know. Just had a burning desire to see it."

"Are the lights on out there?"

"I had a flashlight. Of course, that's with my purse, shoes and laptop now."

"What did you get out of the visit? Did the ghosts of past St. Regis family members clue you in on what you should do with the house?"

"No, but whatever I do is going to be a monumental feat. The place is a mess."

Dylan swung into the parking lot of the Sea View. He'd have expected Mia to stay at one of the more luxurious hotels in town or along the coast. The Sea View was decidedly low rent.

"Oh, crud." Mia slapped the seat. "I don't even have a key to get into my room."

"Stop at the front desk. I'll vouch for you."

They crowded into the small office and tapped the bell on the counter. Gladys Hofstedter came out of the back, and shut the door on the TV blaring behind her. Her eyes popped when she took in the occupants at the counter. "Hello, Mia, Chief Reese."

Looked like Mia didn't need him to vouch for her. She and Gladys were already on a first-name basis. "Hello, Gladys." She folded her arms on the counter. "You're not going to believe this, but the brakes on my rental car went out, and my car went off a cliff near Coral Cove Drive."

Gladys gasped and covered her mouth. "Are you okay?"

"Chief Reese got there just in time." Mia patted his arm. "But all my stuff was in that car—purse, money, credit cards, room key."

"Well, that's not a problem, dear." Gladys pulled

open a drawer and fished out a key with a white tag on it. "You can have this one."

Mia jiggled the key in her palm. "Thanks, Gladys, and don't worry about the money. I'm good for it."

Gladys's plump cheeks turned pink. "I know you are, dear, and isn't it nice to have another Chief Reese at the helm? He's not back one month and he's performing rescues."

The skin on the back of Dylan's neck prickled with heat. He knew taking Dad's place in Coral Cove would come with its challenges, but he didn't figure being treated like some kind of returning hero was one of them…especially since he was far from that.

Mia clenched the key in her fist and banged the counter. "Yep, I'm glad his tenure coincided with my visit."

"Well, I'm going to get back to my show." Gladys made a half turn toward the door that led to her living quarters. "If you need anything else, just let me know."

Reaching for a small refrigerated case, Dylan said, "How about a couple of sodas?"

"You can have those on the house, Chief." Gladys winked.

"Not allowed to take a bribe, Gladys." Dylan shoved his hand in his pocket, drew out three crumpled bills and dropped them onto the counter. "That about do it?"

"That's fine." Gladys swept the money into her hand and shuffled back toward the closed door. "Have a nice evening."

"Since you're not hungry, how about a drink?" Dylan held out one of the bottles to Mia.

"That'll do. Thanks."

He gestured around the motel office. "I can't believe every other hotel in town was booked up, what with the tourist season coming to an end."

Mia shrugged and twisted the cap off her soda. "Almost every other hotel in town is a chain. Gladys worked for my grandparents once, and she's trying to stay in business."

He choked on his soda and it fizzed in his nose. Mia St. Regis had a few compassionate bones left in her body? She'd been that way as a girl, although her imperious attitude sometimes overruled her compassion. The last time he'd briefly seen her in Coral Cove, the summer her boyfriend ran off with her twin, she'd seemed...brittle. And that was even before Marissa absconded with the boyfriend.

She quirked an eyebrow at him. "Don't believe everything you read about me. I thought you knew me better than that."

He held open the door for her and inhaled her expensive perfume as she brushed past him. "I used to know you."

"I'm the same old Mia."

He followed the sway of her hips and the swirl of her skirt around her thighs as she strolled outside. She perched on the seawall and crossed her legs, swinging one slim stem back and forth in a hypnotic rhythm.

He straddled the wall and took another swig of soda. The sea breeze tossed Mia's dark hair and carried a hint of jasmine from the untidy bushes that scrambled along the base of the seawall. For the first time in a long time, knots unraveled in his shoulders and his jaw didn't ache from tension.

She pointed the neck of her bottle at the ocean, a deep, inky-blue relieved by lines of whitecaps on the horizon. "This is another reason why I wanted to stay here. Can't beat this view, and you don't have to share it with a patio full of drunks like you do at the ritzy places down the coast."

"Are you going to turn Columbella House into another hotel with patios for drunks?"

"I'm not sure what I'm going to do yet."

"Holt shouldn't have written that article in the *Herald* about you. It got some people riled up."

She took a sip of soda, and he tried not to fixate on the way her lips wrapped around the bottle.

"So what is it the good residents of Coral Cove want me to do with Columbella House?"

He lifted a shoulder. "Depends on who you ask. Some of the younger people and new business owners would like to see you turn the property into a resort. A lot of the older folks want to see the house restored to its former glory and the land untouched."

"I guess nobody's in favor of me just pushing the whole damned thing into the sea, huh?"

"Oh, I don't know." He stretched his legs in front of him. "I could name a few people who'd like to see the place disappear."

"And you?" She tapped his boot with her toe. "Do you have a preference?"

"It *has* been a magnet for crime lately, but whatever you decide is fine with me. It's your place."

"Not yet it isn't."

The loud, male voice cut through the night air. Mia scrambled to her feet, gasping.

Instinct had Dylan's hand hovering over his holster.

The owner of the voice, an angular man of medium height, stepped into the splash of light Gladys had rigged above the path to the seawall, and Mia stiffened beside Dylan, every fiber of her body vibrating like an electric power line.

"What the hell are you doing here? Following me across the country isn't going to change my mind."

"Just want to make sure I get a piece of what's rightfully mine."

"You already got that."

Everything in Mia's stance and voice screamed anxiety…fear. Dylan faced the intruder, crossing his arms over his chest. "Who is this man, Mia?"

The man turned his sneering face toward Dylan. "Oh, is this the lawman you were always pining for?"

A muscle ticked in Dylan's jaw, and he took a step forward. "Mia?"

"Th-this is my husband."

Chapter Three

Her admission had Dylan expanding his muscles even more until she thought his shirt would rip off his back Incredible Hulk style.

"*Ex*-husband."

Peter flashed his white teeth in a smile that looked more like a snarl. "Not yet, cupcake. I haven't signed those papers."

She squared off against him, digging her toes into the dirt, wishing she had on her high heels. "You'd better get to it then, Peter, or else you'll wind up with nothing."

"We'll see about that. My attorney's working on a big surprise for you."

Dylan stepped in front of her, blocking her view of Peter. She'd rather stare at Dylan's broad back than Peter's weasel face, any day.

"Get moving."

Mia had heard that tone from Dylan before, and it brooked no argument, but this time it carried an edge of…violence. She shivered at the distinct chill in the air.

"Wh-what are you going to arrest me for, *Sheriff*? I'm just enjoying the night air like you two."

Peter had tried to keep the sneer in his voice, but he definitely must've felt the chill, too, his words almost ending in a plea.

"Trespassing. This is private property."

"How do you know I didn't just book a room here?"

"Because Mia booked all the vacant rooms for privacy." Dylan took another step forward and placed his hand on the butt of his gun. "Get lost."

"Ooh, what are you going to do, shoot me for trespassing?"

Something in Dylan's face must've given Peter the idea he just might. He spun around on his expensive shoes and called over his shoulder, "This isn't over, Mia."

She poked her head around Dylan's impressive frame and heaved a sigh when she saw the last of Peter round the corner. "Thank you."

Then she sucked in another breath and held it as she stared at Dylan's straight back. What would he think about her marriage, especially once he knew the reason behind it?

He turned toward her, his blue eyes dark and unreadable, his expression slightly amused. "How'd you wind up married to a tool like that?"

She coughed, her hand covering her mouth and

hiding her smile. Leave it to Dylan to distill the situation to its purest form. "You don't want to know."

"Sure I do, but tell me in your room. It's getting chilly out here, and you don't even have any shoes on." He took her arm and his touch spread warmth throughout her body.

No wonder she could never fully commit to Peter, or any man. She'd always compared the men she'd dated to Dylan Reese, and they'd always come up short.

But Dylan had changed. Would the Dylan of her childhood have accepted the news of her marriage so calmly? She hadn't noticed one drop of judgment in his face or his voice. Growing up as the Coral Cove police chief's son, Dylan had held himself to a higher standard than everyone else.

Not that she could ever live up to it.

She picked her way over the rocky path to the rooms, and then Dylan curled an arm around her waist and swept her off her feet. "I hope you have several pairs of shoes in your room, or you'll need to get tougher feet."

With Dylan's arms around her, gathered close to his body, Mia momentarily lost her capacity for speech…for rational thought. She dropped her head to his shoulder and breathed in his masculine scent, clean and outdoorsy.

Her eyelashes fluttered against his neck and he tightened his grip. Oh, Lord, she'd missed this man. But she'd returned to Coral Cove to take care of business, not to tempt a man she'd written off as too good for her.

Nothing had changed. Now in addition to her other faults, she'd added a divorce. That made her not only unworthy of the police chief but damaged goods.

She kicked her legs as they neared her room. "I thought you knew me better than that, Dylan Reese. Where would I be without at least ten pairs of shoes?"

"Do they all have sky-high heels like that last pair? Because you looked a little overdressed for Coral Cove."

"Then it's a good thing I lost them." She twirled the key chain around her finger, but he still didn't put her on her feet, even though they now stood on smooth cement.

He snatched the key from her hand and unlocked the door. Kicking it open, he carried her across the threshold.

"I don't think Gladys is going to appreciate you kicking her doors."

Releasing his hold on her, he grinned. "Gladys is a romantic. She'd appreciate the circumstances."

Romance? He'd rescued her from a car about to tumble over the side of a cliff, stood up for her against Peter and literally swept her off her feet and carried her over a threshold. Yeah, that all added up to romance...or at least several selfless gestures.

"So spill." He parked himself in an uncomfortable-looking chair, as if preparing for an interrogation. "How'd you end up married to Peter...?"

"Casellas." She dropped to the bed, bouncing up and down for a few seconds, wondering how much she should tell him. "You know the story about how I showed up here in Coral Cove with a boyfriend, Raoul, whom my sister promptly stole from me."

He crossed an ankle over his knee. "Yeah. I was here for about two minutes when you arrived. Marissa was engaged to Tyler Davis at the time—*Mayor* Tyler Davis now, who happens to be the biggest pain in my... Go on."

"Well, after they ran off, I hightailed it out of here, and a lot of people figured I'd had my heart broken."

"I didn't figure that when I heard about it."

"No?" A warm flush crept up her throat. Did Dylan realize nobody could break her heart because she'd kept it wrapped up in gauze for him?

"You're not the running kind and you're not the heartbroken kind. But keep going."

She scooped in a breath and allowed her words to tumble out as she released it. "I left because I had to find someone else to marry."

He raised one eyebrow. He didn't even look shocked. "Because...?"

"Because marriage was one of the terms of my... our inheritance."

He raised the other eyebrow. "Your grandparents stuck that in there?"

"Yes."

"And this Raoul, he was your first victim?"

She reached back, grabbed a pillow and chucked it at him. "You make me sound like a black widow."

"If you had to get married, why the hell didn't you...find someone more appropriate?"

Her pulse quickened. Had he been about to say why hadn't she asked *him?* She'd thought about it, but she hadn't wanted to snare him that way. "That's what I thought I did when I returned to New York and married my friend Peter."

"Prenup?"

"Absolutely."

"Is that what he's trying to weasel out of right now?"

"Right again."

He yawned and stretched his long legs in front of him. "Peter didn't turn out to be much of a friend, did he?"

"He's a photographer. He'd worked on a few of my fashion shows. I knew he wanted to set up his own shop and needed the capital, so I offered him a deal and he jumped at it. We'd dated a few times, but the marriage was in name only, and when I'd satisfied the terms of my grandparents' will and it was time to call it quits, Peter got greedy."

"Marissa had the same requirement?"

This time the flush spread from Mia's neck and suffused her face. "I-it was kind of a competition."

"Let me get this straight." He hunched forward,

gripping his knees. "You and Marissa were in a race to get married to get your hands on Columbella?"

"Sort of." She bit the inside of her cheek. "It's not like we were going to be cut off from our inheritance if we didn't get married, it's just that the first to marry got the house."

He snorted and collapsed back in his chair. "Draconian. Is that why Marissa hooked up with that stick Tyler Davis?"

"Yep—the only reason. When I heard about their engagement, I rushed back here and, and..." She flopped back on the bed, allowing her hair to sweep across her hot face.

She heard a rustle and then the mattress dipped. Dylan's low voice reverberated close to her ear. "Mia St. Regis, are you telling me you brought your boy toy Raoul to Coral Cove to tempt your sister away from marriage with Tyler Davis?"

"Umm, maybe."

He hooked a finger around several strands of hair and pulled them aside like a curtain. "You're unbelievable."

She sat up, almost bumping her head against his chin. "I had to, Dylan. You knew Marissa. She had no feeling for the old place. If she'd have gotten her hands on it, she'd have auctioned off Columbella House to the highest bidder."

"Instead of allowing it to fall into disrepair?"

Her face got even hotter and she dropped her

chin to her chest. "I never meant for that to happen. It's just that after everything—Marissa running off and disappearing and my hasty marriage to Peter—it turned out to be a hollow victory."

"I could've told you that."

"But you weren't around then." And if he had been? Would she have taken a chance and suggested marriage to her old friend? No. Dylan had too much honor for that.

She puffed out her cheeks and expelled a long sigh. "I don't expect you to understand. You'd never do anything to compromise your standards."

Dylan tensed and shifted away from her. "I'm not judging you, Mia. I know that house meant a lot to you at one time, and yes, Marissa would've sold it faster than she would've cheated on Tyler."

She spread her hands. "Anyway, that's my sordid tale. After Marissa ran off with Raoul, ending her engagement to Tyler, I rushed back to New York and made my proposal to Peter. He agreed, and the rest is history."

"Except Peter is no longer happy with the deal he inked."

"Exactly."

"And your twin took off to live the good life with Raoul."

Mia clamped her bottom lip between her teeth and stared out the hotel window into the darkness.

"Mia?" Dylan touched her hand and she jumped.

"What's wrong? Did Marissa find out you'd tricked her, and decided to hold a grudge?"

"I don't know." Her nose stung and she rubbed it with the back of her hand. "I haven't heard from Marissa since she left."

His dark brows snapped together. "She cut you out of her life completely? I know you two were never close, especially for twins, but that seems harsh."

"Oh, she sent several postcards, but no phone calls, no emails."

"Were the postcards nasty?"

"Not really. She never mentioned my scheme. I've tried searching for her online, and I hired a private investigator a few years ago. He took my money and came up empty. I've even tried to find Raoul, but it seems he went back to Brazil. I assumed Marissa went with him."

"That's strange. Marissa had a lot of faults, but holding grudges didn't seem to be among them."

Your sister is dead.

Could she open up to Dylan? When couldn't she? In the old days, she'd been open with Dylan with just about everything except her true feelings for him.

She raked her hair back with her fingers. "It is strange, isn't it? And what's stranger… Did your sister ever tell you she'd found a diary belonging to Marissa a few months ago when she was in Coral Cove with her son?"

Two red spots colored Dylan's cheekbones. "No. I wasn't in touch with Devon at that time. I'm just glad Kieran Roarke had come back from the dead in time to help her and Michael."

Mia tilted her head. Dylan and Devon had always been the close twins in town. "Well, she *did* find Marissa's diary, but before she had a chance to read it or send it to me, it disappeared. And before that, Michelle Girard contacted me about a bracelet she found at Columbella. Michelle's mother used to make them, and Marissa had one she rarely removed."

Swinging her legs over the side of the bed, her blood pumping now, she sat forward. "And finally, Kylie Grant, you know, Rosie the fortune-teller's daughter, she sent me an email that said—"

She choked to a stop. This all sounded crazy. Only bad things had come out of her desire to own Columbella House, and now she was just projecting more guilt on to herself.

Dylan ran a strong, warm hand up her back. "What did the email say?"

"'Your sister is dead.'"

"That's a nice email to send someone, a crazy email." He lightly clasped her neck and circled his thumb against her skin.

"That's not all she wrote in the email. Kylie was here on a case. She works for the FBI and police departments sometimes to help find missing people. While she was—" she waved her hands in the air "—in some kind of trance or something, she felt that Marissa was dead."

"And you believe that mumbo jumbo?"

"Not usually, but Kylie did find that girl who had gone missing from the Coral Cove Music Festival a few years ago."

"That happened right before I got here, and Kylie didn't exactly find the woman. The woman's killer led Kylie to where he'd stashed the body with the intent of doing the same thing to her."

"He'd stashed the body in the walls of Columbella House." Mia shivered and clenched her teeth.

Dylan draped his arm around her shoulder and pulled her snug against his body. "I can have my buddy locate Marissa. He's a P.I. In fact, he worked the case with Kylie. Matt Conner, do you remember him?"

She nodded, trying not to press her body against his solid frame and soak up all his warmth. She turned her head, dangerously close to finding his shoulder again, and her gaze collided with a wavy blue line from a tattoo peeking from the long sleeve of his shirt.

She traced the swirl with the tip of her finger and he winced as if in pain. "When did you get this?"

"A few years ago."

She shoved his sleeve up to get a better view, but the cuff stuck on his forearm. She could see that the blue tail-end of the tattoo curled around his wrist, ending in an arrow pointing to his palm. "What is it?"

Pinching his sleeve between two fingers, he yanked it down. "Another time. It's getting late. You're probably going to be sore from the accident. Do you have some ibuprofen?"

"Plenty."

His arm slid from her shoulder. "Then take it and get some rest. That guy Peter...your ex...husband, he's not going to try anything, is he?"

"He's harmless, just annoying."

Dylan pushed up from the bed, and she jumped up next to him, putting her hand on his arm. "Thanks for everything today, Dylan. Just like old times, when you used to come to rescue me and Devon."

The arm beneath her fingers tensed, and a storm passed across his blue eyes. "Just happened to be in the right place at the right time."

He bent over and kissed her on the forehead. Even that affectionate gesture left a scorching imprint of his lips on her skin.

At the door he turned. "You might want to book up all the vacant rooms in this motel so I don't look like a liar."

"Believe me, this isn't Peter's style. Just another empty threat on his part. He has plenty of those to spare."

"Take care. I guess we'll be seeing each other around town...as long as you're here."

"Maybe I can buy you dinner some night."

"Looking forward to it." He smacked the door-jamb and ambled away.

Mia snapped the door closed and leaned against it. Maybe she should've taken him up on his dinner offer tonight. That way she could've spent more time with him.

At least he hadn't laughed about her suspicions about Marissa. That was Dylan—always willing to listen.

She pushed away from the door and strolled to the bathroom, her head in the clouds. She was not here to reconnect with Dylan Reese. She hadn't even realized he'd be here. Devon hadn't written much about her brother when she'd sent Mia that email about the diary.

Rolling her shoulders, she winced. She'd better get that ibuprofen. She'd be sore for sure tomorrow. A bath might ease her muscles, too. She cranked on the hot water in the tub, letting it run over her fingers.

A large thump at the door almost had her pitching face-first into the bathwater. Had Dylan forgotten something?

She rushed to the door and pulled it open, Dylan's name on her lips. The word died away on a hitched breath.

There was nobody at the door, but whoever had knocked left her a present—a doll. She'd never liked dolls, even when she'd been doll-age appropriate.

She stooped down to snatch the toy from the cement and gasped. This was no ordinary doll. Someone had cut the photo of her out of the paper and glued it over the doll's face, and added one more touch…a needle through the doll's heart.

Chapter Four

Mia clutched her hand to her heart as if she felt the prick of the needle. Stepping back, she banged her elbow on the doorjamb, and pain radiated down her arm. Her gaze darted back and forth along the cement walkway through the bushes.

"Peter?" Her voice broke, and she cleared her throat. "Peter, is that you?"

A rustling of bushes answered her, and beads of sweat broke out on her forehead despite the cool breeze from the ocean. She backed into her room and slammed the door. She scraped the battered chain into place, twitching the curtains at the window for a final peek outside.

Coward.

If Peter thought he'd be getting any more money out of her by playing childish games, he'd better put away whatever it was he'd been smoking.

Pinching the doll by the leg, she dangled it in front of her face. The other soft limbs flopped up and down, and the doll's blue gingham skirt slipped over its head, the head with Mia's face pinned to it. She'd seen these dolls before. An artist up the coast made them and sold them to shops in the neighboring towns.

Lots of people had them, but Peter would've had to buy the doll here in Coral Cove. It would be easy enough to track that down and nail him. She didn't know if he'd broken any laws by dropping a voodoo doll on her doorstep…but Dylan would know.

Her gaze slid to the telephone by the bed. She knew he was off duty, but police chiefs in small towns like Coral Cove never went off duty. Someone at the station could rouse the chief.

She shook the doll again and then dropped it on the table by the window. She couldn't go running to Dylan every time someone yelled *boo* in her face. She'd played that game enough when they were kids, just to see Dylan come running to her rescue.

But she didn't play games anymore. She'd learned her lesson. The last game she'd played had been bringing Raoul to Coral Cove with her, knowing Marissa wouldn't be able to resist his boy-model good looks and sexy accent. Look where that had gotten her.

Saddled with a house she no longer wanted and estrangement from her twin. Surely the only price she had to pay was Marissa's estrangement…not her death.

She shivered as her gaze glanced off the discarded doll, limbs askew, needle through her heart.

Surely not death.

THE NEXT MORNING, Mia followed up with the rental car company after Dylan's report of the accident the night before. Their solicitousness made Mia's teeth ache, but an agent personally delivered a fresh car to the Sea View Motel.

Driving into town, Mia stomped on the brakes a few times just to test them out. She didn't have her driver's license, but she figured Chief Reese would show some understanding.

She pulled into a public parking lot and fed some quarters into the meter. Emerging onto Main Street, she scanned the storefronts, looking for the little touristy knickknack places.

Mia stepped into the first one, the bell on the door dancing in a frantic jingle as she swept into the shop. A tidy woman with a long gray braid down her back looked up from her dusting.

Her ready smile faded and she pursed her lips. "Can I help you?"

Great. Seemed her reputation preceded her everywhere. She may as well have a bull's-eye painted on her forehead.

She practiced her sweetest smile. "Hello, I was wondering if you could help me out."

The woman grunted.

"Do you carry these dolls?" Mia marched forward and thrust the floppy doll, picture on its face and needle in its heart, under the clerk's nose.

The woman jerked back and took a sharp breath. "Is this some kind of joke?"

"Yeah, apparently on me." Mia waved the doll. "You know what kind it is...Cassie's Creations."

Wiggling her fingers, the clerk reached out her hand. "Let me see that. I do carry some of Cassie's Creations."

Mia happily relinquished the squishy doll, wiping her hands on the seat of her white slacks after handing it over.

The woman flipped the doll over and pulled up her skirt. She pushed her glasses up her nose, bringing the doll close to her face. "Yep, it's Cassie's and we do carry these."

"Do you have any?"

"You want another one?"

"I'm trying to find out who bought this one."

"I sold out at the end of the tourist season a few weeks ago." She straightened the doll's skirt and handed it back to Mia. "You might try May's Place across the street. She carries them, too."

Mia tucked the doll under her arm, careful to avoid the end of the needle. "Okay, thanks for your help."

"So what are you going to do with it?"

"Probably take it to the police."

The woman rolled her eyes. "Not the doll, I'm talking about Columbella House."

Mia paused with her hand on the doorknob. "What would you like me to do with it?"

"I'm not sure, but you need to take care of that mess." She puffed at a strand of gray hair that had come loose from her braid. "Maybe the whole thing should've burned down in that fire earlier this summer. There's bad karma when a place is acquired through nefarious methods."

Mia's heart flipped. Did this woman know what Mia had done to obtain the house? "Nefarious methods?"

"I've heard stories about your great-grandfather, and I didn't even grow up here."

"Don't believe everything you hear." *Because sometimes it's worse.* "You have a great day."

Mia snapped the door harder than she'd intended, anxious to escape any more accusations. She spun around on the sidewalk, head down, intent on reaching the next store, and collided with a solid shoulder.

She'd know that shoulder anywhere.

"Dylan!"

He caught her arm. "What's your hurry? Did you just rob Sadie's place?"

She shoved her arms behind her, the legs of the doll tapping the backs of her thighs. "Ah, no. Just looking around."

He cocked his head, his eyes unreadable behind his dark sunglasses. "In a touristy knick-knack shop?"

Shoving out a breath, she whipped the doll from behind her back and jiggled it in front of Dylan. "Someone left this on my hotel doorstep last night."

"What?" He snatched the doll from her and poked at the needle with his fingertip. "Does your soon-to-be ex practice voodoo?"

"Not that I know of, but Peter showed only his good side before I married him." She jerked her thumb over her shoulder at the shop. "I was just checking in there to see if someone matching Peter's description bought a doll recently."

"And now you're going across the street to check the other shop?"

"That's the plan."

"I'll come with you."

Mia was hoping he'd say that. She might get a better reception with the chief of police by her side.

As they crossed the street together, it seemed like half the pedestrians crisscrossing Main Street had a word or a smile for Dylan, their new chief of police. They barely gave her a glance. It was like the living embodiment of *Beauty and the Beast*... only she was the Beast.

The owner of the next shop had propped open her door, and Dylan gestured Mia through first. The woman behind the counter started gushing before they took two steps inside.

"Chief Reese—I can't tell you how good that sounds—what can I do for you today?"

"Good morning, Ellen." He tugged the doll out of Mia's hand. "Have you sold any of these lately?"

"There's a pin in that doll." The woman pursed her lips and her right eye twitched.

Did she assume Mia had defaced the doll? Mia took a breath, but Dylan stilled her with a glance from his blue eyes.

"Exactly." He placed the doll on the counter like it was an injured patient. "That's why we need to know who bought it."

Ellen nudged the doll with the back of her hand. "I had three of these in stock and I sold two this summer. The most recent one to a man, said he was buying it for his daughter."

With her heart pounding, Mia scrambled through the big canvas bag she'd grabbed to substitute as a purse today. She dragged out a dog-eared photography magazine and flipped to the page with the creased corner with the article about Peter. Flattening it on the counter next to her voodoo-doll likeness, she jabbed at a picture of Peter. "Did this man buy the doll?"

Ellen smoothed the picture with her thumb. "I can't tell. I don't think so."

"But it could've been?" Mia pushed the magazine closer to Ellen just in case.

"I suppose so." She shrugged. "What's this about, Chief Reese?"

"Someone making threats against Ms. St. Regis."

"Why? You haven't decided what you're going

to do with Columbella House yet, have you?" Ellen narrowed her eyes.

"Not yet." Mia picked up the doll and shook it. "But stunts like this are not going to win me over."

Dylan thanked Ellen and steered Mia out of the store. He faced her on the sidewalk. "Are you going to confront Peter about this?"

"Of course. I'm not going to allow him to play games like this. The prenup he signed is ironclad."

"Why's he fighting it now? Greed?"

"That and—" she smacked the rolled-up magazine against her palm "—the fact that his business is failing."

Dylan pushed up his sunglasses and rubbed his eyes. "Mia, Mia. The things you get into—nothing's changed."

A lot had changed. Mia studied Dylan's strong hands and his square, resolute chin. She'd never take him for granted again. She'd grown up in the shadow of this boy becoming a real man, and she hadn't met a real man since she'd left Coral Cove.

She smiled at her reflection in his dark glasses. "I'm not as wild as I used to be—I promise."

"You haven't been in town two days and ex-husbands are leaving creepy dolls on your doorstep and your car is careening off a cliff." He snapped his fingers. "That reminds me. Your purse and laptop case were thrown clear of the car when it crashed. My guys recovered them and I have them at the station."

She clapped her hands. "That's the best news I've had all day…that and the rental car company's willingness to deliver a new car to me."

"Do you want to walk to the station with me?"

"Absolutely." She took his arm, her fingertips pressing against the solid muscle beneath his khaki uniform shirt. "Walking with you is like being under this protective umbrella."

"You feel like you need a protective umbrella?"

"Yeah, from all the slings and arrows being sent my way from the good folks of Coral Cove."

He bumped her shoulder. "You're being paranoid. Like Ellen said, you haven't indicated which way you're leaning on a decision for Columbella."

"I'm going out there today. I already called the electric company to have the electricity turned on."

"Do you want me to go with you?"

"Can you?" She squeezed his arm. "You're not busy?"

"This is Coral Cove."

She snorted. "Tell that to Chief Evans, the guy who just left. Murders, suicides, kidnappings. I think there's been more crime here this past summer than all the years your dad was chief."

"Weird, huh? And all of it ending up at Columbella House. That's what has people on edge about the house."

"I don't blame them. What did you call it earlier? A magnet for crime? Even before this summer, it was a magnet for a whole lot of other things." A tremble rolled through her body and she jostled closer to Dylan.

He charged through the doors of the police station like he owned the place. Hunching over the front desk, he called out, "Hey, Clark, do you have Ms. St. Regis's stuff from the car crash?"

An officer came out from the back, hugging a gray bin to his chest. "Got it right here. You're one lucky lady."

"Don't I know it."

He placed the bin on the counter and slid it toward her. The odors of gasoline and burning tires wafted from her purse and laptop case.

"Ugh. I hope the contents are salvageable because I'm going to have to throw these bags away."

"Do you want me to take those to your car and then follow you over to Columbella?"

"I don't want to take up your time, Dylan, if you have other work to do."

"I've been meaning to go out there anyway—a couple of things I wanted to check out."

Dylan shoved the bin into her trunk and closed it with a snap. "If you need help retrieving anything on that hard drive, let me know. There's a guy in town, a teacher, who's good with computers."

She leaned against the car door with her hands grasping the door handle behind her. *He must think I'm still a total ditz.*

"I appreciate it, Dylan, but you don't have to hold my hand every step of the way. Believe it or not, I actually live on my own and manage to eat and pay my bills and everything."

As soon as the words were out of her mouth, she wanted to bite her tongue. Two red spots stained his cheekbones, and his jaw tightened.

"Just trying to help out."

Pushing off the car, she grabbed his forearm, her fingers slipping up his sleeve to caress the mysterious tattoo.

"I'm sorry. I sounded ungrateful. I just want to let you know I'm not that silly girl who used to run to you for help killing a spider...or to tell some overeager teenage boy to back off."

His lips quirked up at one end as he stepped away from her touch. "Guess I'm still overprotective. Do you still want me to meet you at Columbella?"

"Y-yes. Of course."

"Tell you what. You go ahead and I'll meet you over there in a bit."

"Sounds good." Mia pasted on a cheery smile and then slumped in the car when he walked away. *Damn, girl. Why are you pushing away the one good thing left in this town?*

Mia drove up the coast with the window down, allowing the wind to tangle the strands of her hair. She eyed the rearview mirror more than a few times, hoping to catch a glimpse of Dylan's squad car following her. He'd wanted to come along, but she'd implied she wanted him to back off.

Did she?

Not at all. She just wanted Dylan to take her seriously now. She'd gotten off to a bad start by being forced to confess how she'd set up Marissa and married Peter just to get her hands on a house. No wonder he felt she still needed saving from herself.

Coral Cove Drive looked a lot less spooky by daylight. The house didn't look much better, though. In fact, it looked worse. It didn't even have that haunted vibe going for it in the harsh light of day that exposed all its flaws and blemishes.

She rolled to a stop in front of the house and scrambled out, dragging her canvas bag with her. She pushed open the front door and poked her head inside before entering.

She expelled a sigh of relief when she saw the broken wood hanging from the balustrade. That was what she'd seen last night; that was what sent her scurrying for safety. Not that her rental car had proved to be safe.

She wrinkled her nose at the dust and decay in the house. Could anyone ever really restore the house? Would she want anyone to restore it?

She wandered around the downstairs, taking notes on a yellow legal pad. She jiggled the handle of the basement door, dreading the trip downstairs. Then decided to put it off for another time.

She climbed the stairs like she had lead weights on her feet. Reaching the second-story landing, she peered over the railing. Why exactly had she wanted this house?

Why had she wanted it enough to trick her sister and marry a man she didn't love? Had she really expected Dylan to offer himself in Peter's stead?

She threw open the doors to all the bedrooms and bathrooms. After taking inventory of the items in these rooms, she dragged herself up to the third floor.

Rosie Grant, the mother of Kylie Grant, the same psychic who had sent her the email about Marissa, had hung herself from the third-floor landing a few years ago.

Mia shivered and scooted past the spot where Rosie had jumped. But more terror awaited her at the end of the hallway. A gaping hole was all that remained of the cavity where some local man had walled up a body.

What was it about this place? It drove people to madness.

She took more notes on the third floor, and then sank into a chair, facing a set of double doors that opened on to a balcony facing the sea.

Crossing her arms behind her head, she stretched her legs in front of her. The only thing that made sense right now was Dylan Reese. If he wanted to play knight in shining armor, who was she to stop him?

But she didn't want them to fall into their old, familiar pattern. She wanted him to see her in a new light, for the woman she'd become. Because now maybe she could meet him on equal footing.

She cocked her head. She could hear a rumbling of voices raised above the rush of the ocean beneath her.

Unless the Vincents were having one heck of a big party, there couldn't be that many people gathered on this block.

She peeled herself from the chair and scuffed to the balcony. Here the voices came cascading along the sea breeze. Shouts. Yells. Jeers.

Mia jogged down the spiral stairs that led from the balcony to the rocks and then made her way to the front of the house.

She stumbled to a halt, her jaw dropping. Hordes of people were gathered around Columbella House, carrying signs and yelling at each other.

Then a few of them spotted her and started yelling at her. She set her jaw and marched to the front of the house.

She zeroed in on the closest person. "What is going on? What are you people doing here?"

"We just want to make sure you do the right thing."

Before Mia had a chance to respond, another person pushed her way forward and wagged her finger. "Don't try to force yourself in here and influence her."

Sirens sliced through the air, but the noise didn't faze the crowd. Two police cars pulled up to the curb, and Mia blew out a breath when she saw Dylan climb out of one of the cars. He cut a swath through the mob, and they parted for him.

"What's going on here?"

Mia flung out her arms. "I was inside, and apparently, these people just spontaneously gathered here."

He flicked a sign next to him. "Doesn't look spontaneous to me."

"This is a peaceful protest, Chief," a voice yelled from the back of the crowd.

"It doesn't look peaceful to me, and unless someone can produce a permit, you're going to have to disperse."

A low chant started slowly. "Restore, restore, restore, restore."

Another thrumming began from the other side. "Rebuild, rebuild, rebuild, rebuild."

The words merged in a hissing and bubbling cacophony. The faces swam before Mia so that they no longer resembled people but just working mouths and angry eyes.

Then out of nowhere, an object came hurtling from the belly of the crowd and Mia felt a sting on her chin.

Chapter Five

Mia staggered against his shoulder and gasped. Dylan's arm went around her like second nature. "Are you okay?"

She turned a pale face to him and blood dripped from her chin next to the scuff from the air bag.

"What the hell?"

Touching the wound with trembling fingers, she said, "Someone threw something."

Dylan scanned the ground and saw a sharp-edged rock at Mia's feet. Anger coursed through his veins. "Baxter, get these people out of here."

He tucked Mia against his side and guided her to the dilapidated porch while his officers began blasting at the crowd through bullhorns.

Dylan held up the rock. He didn't need a bullhorn. "If I find out who threw this rock, I'm bringing you up on assault charges."

The crowd took on a frightened aspect, as if it feared its own strength. Slowly it melted away, but nobody stepped forward with information about who threw the rock.

Dylan crouched beside Mia. "Do you want me to call the paramedics?"

"For a cut on the chin?" She shook her head and her silky, dark hair slipped over her shoulder. "I'm okay."

Why did she have to keep trying to prove her toughness to him? He'd known her since childhood, and she'd always been a leader with a spine of steel. Of course, sometimes she'd led her followers, including his sister, into all kinds of craziness, but that only added to her charm.

"I know you don't have running water in that house or anything close to a clean bandage, so you're going to have to get that cleaned up and dressed."

She pointed across the street. "Is Michelle Girard back yet?"

"No, not yet. School doesn't start for another week."

More sirens wailed down the street and an ambulance swung into view. Dylan shrugged. "I guess Officer Brady called it in."

"Those EMTs are going to get tired of being at my beck and call."

"Stop talking. You're making it bleed more."

The paramedics hustled from their van, bags in hand. "Do you need to go to the hospital?"

Mia rolled her eyes, trying to be the tough girl again. "It's just a cut on the chin."

Dylan hefted the rock in his palm. "It was a shot to the face with this. When did you have your last tetanus shot?"

"That's what I'd like to know." The EMT snapped open his bag, all business.

Dylan stepped back and allowed the paramedics to do their jobs. Mia insisted she didn't need to be carted to the hospital, but she sat patiently as they cleaned and dressed her wound.

He eyed the stragglers, as Brady darted among them, notepad in hand. Grady turned to Dylan and shrugged, and Dylan motioned him over.

"Nothing?"

"Nobody is admitting to seeing anything, but I think they all got spooked when their little protest turned violent."

Dylan shoved a hand in his pocket and half turned toward Columbella House. "This house does things to people. Do you believe in evil auras or bad vibes?"

He'd expected his officer to snort at him and call him crazy, but Grady slid a glance at the old house and clenched his jaw.

"Usually not, but this house? Bad news all the way around." He hunched in and cupped a hand around his mouth. "Don't tell anyone, but I'm on the side of the folks who want this thing torn down and turned into a resort hotel."

"You don't think the bad vibes would persist?"

"You have a point there."

"What are you two whispering about?" Mia, a white bandage plastered to her chin, strolled toward them.

Dylan exchanged a guilty look with Grady and then reached out and nudged Mia's chin. "You don't need stitches?"

"It was just a scratch." She rolled up her sleeve. "I did get a shot, though, thanks to you."

He inspected the red dot on her upper arm. "I think the paramedics would've thought of that all on their own."

"Do you have the rock, Chief? Maybe we should take it in as…uh, evidence." Grady colored up to roots of his hair.

Dylan dug the sharp-edged rock from his pocket and held it out. "Sure, but you're not going to get any prints off it, and I don't think anyone's going to step forward and claim it as their very own rock."

Grady took it anyway. "Maybe a witness will come forward in secret. These were all friends and neighbors out here. Nobody's going want to be labeled a rat."

"Even if that rock could've seriously injured Mia?" Dylan shook his head. "If so, this town doesn't have the values it did when I was growing up here."

Grady pocketed the rock and returned to his

squad car. The few remaining onlookers disappeared when the ambulance rounded the corner.

Dylan turned to Mia. "Do you need to go back inside the house?"

"I left my bag in there." She turned and put a tentative foot on the first step of the crumbling porch.

"Sorry I couldn't get here sooner. Uh, police business."

Actually, he didn't have much to do back at the station. Mia had made it clear she didn't want his hovering presence, and he didn't want his own issues to get in the way of his relationship with her.

Relationship? They had no relationship. She'd returned to Coral Cove for business, and she'd be back in New York once she made a decision.

And he'd returned to Coral Cove for...redemption? Whatever his personal reasons, he couldn't drag Mia into the middle of them.

"You *were* here when someone decided to chuck a rock at me, so it wouldn't have made a difference anyway."

"If I had come earlier, I would've seen the protest forming and I would've dispersed the crowd before things got sketchy."

Mia shrugged and picked her way over the last two porch steps. She'd left the front door open, and she pushed at it. The squealing hinges made Dylan clench his teeth.

Light from the open door and the windows

streamed across the floors and shrouded furniture. He sneezed from the dust.

"Pretty bad, huh?" Mia grabbed her canvas bag from a chair and cruised to the front door. "I've had enough for one day."

As Mia locked up, Dylan faced the street and saw a blue compact car squeal around the corner.

"What kind of car is your ex-husband driving?"

"I have no clue." She hitched the big bag over her shoulder. "Why, did you see him?"

"If he's driving a blue compact, yeah." Dylan narrowed his eyes in the direction where the little car huffed off. "Maybe he was here at the protest."

"He could've been. There was a sea of faces out there, all blurred together." She hit the remote on her car and yanked open the driver's side door. "I could see Peter leaving the voodoo doll easier than I could imagine him chucking the rock. Peter is not a rough-and-tumble kinda guy."

"Money can make people do crazy things. Look at you."

Mia had been tossing her bag on to the passenger seat and jerked up at his words. "Wait a minute. I didn't trick Marissa and marry Peter for money… it was for this house."

"And the house doesn't represent money? Who are you kidding, Mia? It sits on a prime piece of beachfront property. I know a few developers who would kill to get their hands on this lot."

She stomped her foot. "It wasn't like that, Dylan.

Both Marissa and I had plenty of money. It was just a game to get the house. And I won."

He ground his teeth together. He hadn't meant to go all judgmental on her. That was the old Dylan. The Dylan who used to believe he could do no wrong. Make no mistake.

That Dylan died with Melody Firenzi.

Dragging in a breath, he traced his fingertip along her bandage. "I know that. You and Marissa always played by different rules, and you both knew those rules."

Mia bit her lip. "I thought we both knew the rules, but then Marissa disappeared. I assumed she'd figured out what I had done and wrote me off."

"Or she never figured it out and felt too ashamed and guilty to contact you while she was having fun with Paolo, the Brazilian Adonis."

She slugged his arm. "His name was Raoul."

"I'm sorry." He held up his hands. "Can I take you out to dinner tonight to make up for accusing you of money lust?"

He held his breath like a boy asking a girl out on a first date. He'd never tried to date Mia. She'd never seemed interested, and he didn't want to get in line to have his heart broken by one of the St. Regis twins. The twins already had a long list.

"Sure, sure, let's grab a bite."

His chest deflated. At least she'd accepted, although she was already downplaying the date's significance. And why shouldn't she? They were two old friends grabbing a bite to eat. She had to eat.

Then she'd go back to New York.

"I'll pick you up at the Sea View around seven."

"Sounds good."

The growl of a car's engine had them both swiveling their heads toward the street. A silver Escalade cruised to a stop at the curb, and Mayor Tyler Davis poked his head out the window.

"Looks like we missed all the excitement."

Mia mumbled under her breath. "Just what I need."

When he cut the engine, a sleek blonde slipped from the car and floated toward them. "We heard what happened, Mia. This is getting out of control."

Linda Davis, the mayor's wife, landed in front of them, her gaze skipping over their shoulders to take in the house.

"Hi, Linda." Mia stuck out her hand. "I was going to call you later to get your advice about the house. Hey, Tyler...er, Mayor."

Davis clicked his tongue. "The situation with the house is getting out of control. You know where I stand, Mia. I'd hate for Coral Cove to lose an historical landmark like Columbella House."

Mia wrinkled her nose. "You don't think there's been enough bad juju associated with the house?"

"Bad juju?" Davis twisted his lips, looking like someone just shoved a lemon in his mouth.

"You know. Bad vibes. Unpleasant aura." Mia waved her arms around.

Davis sniffed. "It's a house—brick and mortar."

"Tyler doesn't have much imagination." Linda patted her husband's sleeve. "I'd be happy to discuss the house with you, Mia. I know a lot of great renovators in the area…if you choose to go that route. I'm also listing the house across the street, so I'll be in the area."

"Thanks, Linda. I'll call you later. I'm ready to get out of here now."

Davis made a move toward his Escalade. "I'm sure you are. I just wanted to make sure our new chief here had everything under control."

When they drove off, Dylan rolled his eyes at Mia. "Doesn't anyone else want the job of mayor?"

"Tyler's been wanting to run this town since he was class president in high school."

"He had a close relationship with the previous chief—daily meetings, fundraisers, briefings—I've been putting him off since I took the job and I don't think he's too happy about it."

"You're a popular chief. He'll have to learn to live with it." Mia slid onto the seat of the car. "Seven o'clock. I'll be ready."

"Drive carefully, and don't pick up any strange dolls."

Mia laughed, but the humor never reached her eyes. "I'm going to hole up in my motel room and see if I can get anything out of my laptop."

She slammed her car door, revved the engine and zipped down the street. He could give her a speeding ticket for that quarter of a mile alone.

His gaze narrowed as he watched her taillights disappear around the corner. Mia had run into a stretch of bad luck or she had gotten accident-prone—or someone didn't want her in Coral Cove.

And it wasn't him.

MIA WAVED TO GLADYS as she passed in front of the office. Gladys flapped her gossip magazine at Mia in greeting.

Mia's gait slowed as she approached the door of her motel room, and she studied the ground. No weird dolls. No rocks. No trip wires.

Peter had really sunk to new lows. He could've just asked her for a loan to prop up his studio. She would've obliged, but not now.

She pushed open the door and fell across the double bed. Gladys's place was in serious need of a major upgrade. What hotel installed double beds in single rooms anymore?

She bounced up from the bed and snagged her battered laptop case from the floor by the door. She pulled out her laptop and scooted back against the headboard, plumping the pillows behind her with one hand.

Firing up the computer, she whispered, "Please, please, please."

The laptop whirred, hiccupped and whirred

some more. She focused on the spinning blue wheel until she got dizzy.

She flopped against the pillows. Served her right for not backing up everything.

The gruesome email from Kylie Grant wasn't the only message she'd been saving. How ironic that within one week, she'd received two emails—one warning of death, the other bringing life.

She sighed and closed her eyes. Dylan mentioned a computer guy in town. She'd have to hit him up for the name tonight.

Dylan Reese to the rescue again...and again.

She didn't believe for a minute she was the only one who was seeing an old friend with new eyes.

The drop-dead gorgeous looks and the rock-hard bod were the same—better than ever. But Dylan had a different aspect about him, softer.

She snorted and dragged a pillow over her face. There was nothing soft about Dylan.

Was he a little less perfect than before? Or was it just that she was seeing him with adult eyes now instead of the hero worship of a girl?

Whatever. Dylan Reese had moved into the realm of the attainable. Now she just needed to decide whether or not she wanted to make a play and risk disappointment and heartache.

Oh, what the hell. What was a little more heartache in this life?

A few hours later, all gussied up, or at least

gussied up for a small coastal town, Mia perched on the edge of the bed, waiting for her date.

As the digital alarm clock clicked over to seven o'clock, the hotel room door rumbled with a knock. Maybe no longer perfect, but prompt.

She swept open the door and drank in her first sight of Dylan out of uniform. His jeans hugged his thighs and his blue T-shirt matched his eyes. His twin sister, Devon, had gotten the blond hair, but Dylan's brown hair had streaks of gold that reflected the California sunshine.

"You're a little overdressed for Coral Cove, but you look great."

She twirled around in her summer dress, nearly tripping in her flip-flops. "This old thing?"

"One of your designs?"

"No, I've had this for years. Probably bought it here." She grabbed a small purse and a sweater. "Where to?"

"Somewhere on the coast?" He placed his hand on the small of her back as they walked through the motel's courtyard. "How'd it go with your laptop?"

"Not good. I'm going to need the computer guy."

"Remind me tonight. I'll give you his number." He opened the door of his truck and she balanced one foot on the runner and hopped onto the seat.

As Dylan slid into the driver's seat, she said, "You always did like your trucks."

"Nothing much has changed."

She slid a gaze to her left. She doubted that. The

blue-and-red tattoo crawling down his forearm was testament to that. She could now see the design—a one and a five, with the curve of the five swirling to his wrist, ending in an arrow.

What the heck did it mean?

He aimed the car down the coast where the twinkling lights outlined the curve of the shoreline.

"No more mishaps?"

"Like I said, I bolted my door, took stock of my purse and laptop and took a quick nap."

"Did that ex of yours contact you?"

"Nope."

"What do you think he hoped to accomplish by leaving that doll for you?"

She adjusted the straps of her sundress beneath her sweater and shrugged. "Intimidation."

Dylan threw back his head and barked out a laugh. "He doesn't know you too well, does he?"

"He's desperate. Desperate people do desperate things."

"Yeah, don't forget that."

They pulled into the front drive of the restaurant, and Dylan left his truck with a valet parking attendant.

Mia pointed to the dark sky with wisps of pink sketched along the horizon. "Looks like we missed the sunset."

"Good, maybe we can get a window seat."

She pinched his side. "Who are you kidding? This town rolled out the red carpet for you when you returned. They'll give you anything, certainly a window seat."

He squeezed her hip. "I don't know. Not when I'm with the town pariah."

His words, meant in jest, caused a frisson of fear to zigzag down her spine. She didn't want to be the town pariah.

His arm curled around her waist and he pulled her close. "I'm just kidding. Half the town is going to love you when you make your decision. The other half is going to have to live with it."

Mia smirked as the hostess fell all over herself finding a window seat for the chief of police.

Dylan ordered a beer and Mia stuck with her old standby, a frozen margarita, the rim caked with salt.

Dylan's eyes darkened to the color of the Pacific Ocean out their window as he watched her lick the salt off the edge of the glass before taking a sip of her drink through the straw.

He swallowed, his Adam's apple bobbing in his throat. "You always did like margaritas...you and Marissa."

She took a bigger gulp of her drink, ignoring the brain freeze. "Where is she, Dylan?"

"Where did her last postcard come from?"

"The south of France."

"So she's in Cote d'Azure?"

"That was last year."

"Haven't heard from her since?"

"No."

"And before that?"

"A year before France, she sent me a postcard from Spain—the Costa del Sol."

"And what does she say in these postcards?"

"Inane, meaningless things—having a great time, don't worry, see you soon."

"Sounds like Marissa—inane and meaningless."

"Ouch."

He skimmed a hand across the table and toyed with her fingers. "You always had more substance than Marissa."

"I just don't understand why she doesn't email me, give me a return address, invite me to join her sometime."

"For twins you two were never that close."

Mia clenched the napkin in her lap. "I'm beginning to realize how far apart we really were."

"Kylie Grant had a feeling Marissa was dead. That doesn't mean a whole lot."

"Kylie Grant is a Gypsy fortune-teller."

Dylan grinned. "Apparently, that Gypsy fortune-teller mesmerized my buddy Matt Conner. They're together now."

"Have you contacted Matt about tracking down my sister yet?"

"Not yet. I know he's working on getting his job back with the LAPD after he was framed."

The waitress interrupted them with a plate of steaming calamari.

Mia plucked a few of the crispy critters from the pile and dropped them on her plate. "And what about you? Aren't you going to miss the big city police department in San Jose?"

"No." Dylan dragged a calamari through some red cocktail sauce on his plate and sucked it into his mouth.

The tattoo on his arm undulated with his flexing muscle, and Mia reached out a slightly greasy fingertip and tapped it.

"Are you ever going to tell me about this? What does the number fifteen signify?"

"I'll tell you about it sometime. Maybe if you stick around long enough."

Was that a bribe to get her to hang around town? His reticence to discuss the tattoo only increased its mystery.

She crunched through another calamari, tilting her head. "You were always a straight shooter. You've got secrets now."

"Doesn't everyone?"

"Yeah, they do." And if he was still holding on to a few of his, she'd hold on to hers.

They polished off the appetizer just in time for their dinners. Secrets forgotten for the time being, they reminisced about growing up in Coral Cove. For Mia, the sexual tension between them receded, and she felt the warmth of reconnecting with an old friend, a friend who knew and understood her roots.

It had been too long.

And the dinner ended too soon.

Dylan started the car and Mia said, "Are you sure the chief of police should be driving after a beer?"

"Umm, one beer for a six-foot-two, one-hundred-and-ninety-pound man as opposed to two margaritas for a five-foot-four, one-hundred-pound woman? I'll take those odds."

"I don't weigh a hundred pounds."

"Whatever. You're tipsy."

"I'm not tipsy."

He pulled onto the highway, and the lights merged into a diffused glow. She squinted and the lights blurred even more. Maybe she *was* tipsy.

He pulled in front of the Sea View Motel. "Is Gladys still on duty?"

"Gladys is always on duty. Since her husband died, she pretty much runs the place on her own."

Dylan held her hand as they followed the path to her motel room. His grasp felt warm and sure and right. Maybe she *would* stick around long enough to discover how he got that tattoo.

They reached the door of her motel room, and Mia turned on her toes, not sure what to expect. Had this been a date? A get-together of old friends? Maybe she should just let Dylan take the lead. She didn't always have to be the one taking charge and making decisions.

A smile touched her lips, natural and spontaneous. "Thanks for dinner."

"My pleasure. It was great...catching up."

She fluttered her fingers toward the courtyard. "I guess if I were staying at a nicer place, we could have a drink in the bar or something."

"I don't need another drink, and neither do you."

Did he just slam the door in her face?

"Umm, you're probably right." She gripped his arm and rose on her tiptoes, planting a kiss on his rough cheek. "Good night, Dylan."

His eyes glowed for a moment like he wanted to devour her. Then he pinched her nose. "Good night, Mimi."

He stepped back as she gave him a halfhearted wave and shut the door. Leaning her hot cheek against the cheap wood, she heard his retreating footsteps.

With that gesture and the childhood nickname, Dylan had doused any flame that had been dancing in the pit of her stomach. He'd made it clear he wanted to keep things platonic.

She could do that.

She kicked her leather flip-flops into the corner and shrugged out of her sweater. She'd better torpedo any romantic thoughts she had about Dylan and get back to business.

The solid rap on her motel room door had her forgetting all her dire warnings to herself, and she flew to answer it.

She flung open the door, ready to throw herself into Dylan's arms. Instead, she faced a squat, beefy man with tangled black hair, a gold-toothed leer and a tattoo just like Dylan's.

Chapter Six

Dylan cruised to the corner in his truck with the window down. He glanced in his rearview mirror at the single headlight from a motorcycle that turned into the Sea View Motel. He accelerated away from the stop sign and buzzed up his window against the noise from his engine.

Engine noise.

Why hadn't he heard any noise from that bike heading into Mia's motel?

He roared up the highway, and then made a U-turn at the first opportunity. With his heart racing as fast as his engine, he careened back down the road toward the Sea View. His truck bounced and jostled as he drove it into the driveway, and he threw it into Park right behind Gladys's old Saab.

And the Harley leaning into its kickstand.

Dylan shoved open his door and jogged down the semilighted path to Mia's room. Her voice rose into the night, sure and strong:

"Get lost."

The adrenaline in Dylan's body pumped into his extremities, putting every muscle on high alert. A low growl rumbled deep in his throat when he spotted the squat figure at Mia's door, his booted foot in the doorjamb, his hand reaching for his waistband.

Dylan's jog turned into a sprint and he hurtled himself at the man, knocking him off balance and sending them both crashing to the ground.

Mia screamed.

The solid form beneath him grunted and cursed. Dylan drew a breath into his tight chest when he met the eyes of Rocco Vick.

Dylan drew back his arm and slugged the scumbag in the jaw. The cracking noise could've been the guy's bone or his head against the cement. Either way, his dull eyes rolled back in their sockets and his mouth slackened, a dribble of blood seeping from the corner.

Dylan shoved his arm against Vick's throat to make sure he was out cold, and then reached for his cell phone to call for backup.

"What's going on, Dylan? Who is he?"

After speaking into the phone, he cranked his head toward Mia's pale face. She was hugging herself and had one leg crossed over the other.

"He's some dirtbag from a motorcycle gang. Dangerous and on parole. Did he hurt you?"

"Didn't have much of a chance. He knocked on my door, I...I answered it, told him he had the wrong room, and he started making advances."

"Advances?" His mouth was so dry he had a hard time speaking.

"You know—started with the lines and tried to shove his way into my room."

"My God, Mia." Dylan pushed to his feet, keeping one shoe on the unconscious man's throat. "Are you okay?"

"Yeah. I had no intention of letting him in my room. I was just about to knee him in the…well, you-know-whats."

Dylan shook his head, the tension seeping from his back and shoulders as the sound of a siren permeated the air.

"Why was he here, Dylan? Do you know him?"

He shifted his gaze to Vick's face and raked it across the numbered tattoo on his forearm. He increased the pressure of his foot on the man's neck.

"Yeah."

The patrol car squealed to a stop, and Gladys's reedy voice filtered down the path. "What's happening?"

Two officers with Gladys bringing up the rear hustled into the courtyard. "Where is he, Chief?"

"Under my foot. I knocked him out. Check him for priors and a parole violation." Dylan nudged the intruder's leg with the toe of his shoe. "He has a knife on him, too."

As the officers worked to bring the man around, Dylan backpedaled Mia into her room and slammed the door behind them. "You don't need to see that."

She grabbed the front of his shirt, bunching the material in her fists. "Okay, stop dancing around now. Who was that guy, how did you know he was here, and most important, why do the two of you have matching tattoos?"

"You noticed that, huh?" He rubbed his hand over the ink on his arm. "I knew I should've tried to have it removed before showing up here."

She dragged him to the bed—not that he hadn't fantasized about this since the minute he laid eyes on her in town—then she pushed him down, dropping next to him on the mattress. "Spill."

For safety's sake, she deserved to know why she'd been accosted, but he didn't have to tell her *everything*. Now was not the time to spoil his image in her eyes.

"That dude is a member of the Fifteenth Street Lords...and so was I."

She sucked in a short breath and squeaked it out. "Were you undercover or something?"

"Exactly."

She traced the lines of the tattoo and he shivered. "Pretty dedicated to the assignment to get this ink job. You couldn't have gotten a henna tattoo or something?"

"I don't think that would've gone over too big with the Lords."

"At least you didn't have to kill someone to prove your loyalty...did you?"

A spasm of pain twisted his gut, but he stretched

his lips into a smile over his clenched teeth. "No, but my cover was blown and…some bad stuff went down."

She pointed an unsteady finger at the door. "Is that why that Neanderthal showed up?"

"Yes." The tightness in his belly increased when he realized he'd brought danger to Mia's doorstep… more danger. Could the Lords have been responsible for the brakes going out on her rental car? They would have liked nothing more than to get revenge on him for infiltrating their little party—and Vick harbored a special hatred toward him.

Even though Dylan had already paid big-time for all of it.

Scooting closer to him on the bed, Mia asked, "Why'd you come back to the motel? How did you know he was here?"

"I noticed the motorcycle in my rearview mirror. A motorcycle with a silent engine."

"So you knew it was one of your old friends."

His back stiffened and he chewed his words. "They're not my friends. Never were."

"I know that." Soothing fingers trailed down his arm. "Just trying to lighten the mood a little so I don't crawl into the bed and pull the covers over my head."

"I'm sorry." He caressed her neck, and her silky hair tickled the back of his hand. "I brought that guy here. He came down here because of me and must've followed me."

She leaned against his touch for a minute before springing up from the bed. Bracing her shoulder against the wall, she peeked out the curtains. "They're gone. What are they going to do with him?"

"Probably turn him over to his parole officer. He'll be heading back to prison, since he just violated about a hundred terms of his parole."

She let the curtain fall back into place and squared her shoulders against the wall. "Will there be more?"

"Maybe." He reclined on the bed, propping himself up with his elbows. "They're not going to kill me or anything—that hit would be too high profile, even for the Lords."

"But they might continue to harass you...and those close to you."

He eased up from the bed and sauntered toward Mia, still holding up the wall. He braced his hands on either side of her head. "Are you close to me?"

The little bow between her breasts on the sundress trembled with the pounding of her heart. Her tongue swept across her lips, moistening them to a glossy pink. "W-we're old friends."

He studied her long, dark lashes fluttering over her eyes and bent his head to brush his lips across her mouth, still tangy from her twin margaritas. The tantalizing chasteness of the kiss sent a jolt of desire through his core, making him hard.

He'd avoided falling under the St. Regis spell

when he'd been a hormonal teen, and now that he was a seasoned adult that spell was dragging him along like a tidal wave.

Leaning her head against the inside of his arm, she sighed. She'd had a rough day—the rock, the parolee—he didn't want to strike while her defenses were down.

He lifted a strand of her hair, rubbing it between his two fingers. "You're tired. You need some sleep."

Her eyelids flew open. "I need...sleep."

He avoided the temptation of tweaking her nose again to put them back on familiar footing. Maybe a little unsteadiness was what they both needed to figure this out.

Dropping another kiss on top of her head, he said, "Lock up, and don't open the door for anyone. Didn't you look out the window first when you opened the door to that thug?"

"I thought it was you. I thought maybe you'd forgotten something." Her dark eyes softened, and he knew if he made a move now he'd find fertile ground for his advances.

"Watch yourself, Mia. I'll try to check up on you tomorrow. And don't go out to that house by yourself anymore."

She nodded. "Thanks for taking out that guy."

He grinned. "Sounded like you were doing a pretty good job of that yourself."

She closed the door behind him and he listened

for the deadbolt. Maybe the Fifteenth Street gang member was behind the brakes and even the rock. The doll? Not the Lords' style.

With Vick locked up, Mia should be safe. Unless she had her own enemies in this town...enemies who pretended to be friends.

THE FOLLOWING MORNING, Mia stopped by the motel office on her way to her new rental car. She poked her head in the door. "You okay, Gladys?"

"I'm okay." She glanced up from her gossip mag and slid her glasses down her nose. "Are you?"

"Couldn't be better." Especially after that smooch from Dylan last night. It didn't count as a full-fledged kiss, but lip-on-lip had to count for something.

"I've never seen so much action around this old place." Gladys tapped her chin. "And I heard someone threw a rock at you yesterday."

"It's just a scratch."

"And the man last night?"

"Someone from Dylan's past, but he showed up in time to take the guy out."

"Chief seems to be spending a lot of time here." She pushed the glasses back up her nose and buried it in the glossy pages of her magazine.

"See you later." Mia practically skipped from the office. For running into a string of bad luck, she sure felt good.

She drove through town and, slowing down,

peered out the window at the addresses on the east-Ohside apartment buildings. Last night, Dylan had given her the phone number of the computer whiz, and the guy, Alec Wright, had asked her to bring the laptop to his place.

Spotting the ceramic numbers on the side of the pink stucco building, she pulled to the curb as a car sped past. She cut the engine and stared after the blue car taking the corner at a high rate of speed. Had that car been following her?

After last night's adventure with the motorcycle goon, she really needed to be more aware of her surroundings.

She slipped from the car and hauled her battered and charred laptop case from the trunk. Her heart skipped at the sound of another car engine behind her, and she twirled around, her fight-or-flight instinct in high gear.

She let out her breath with a whoosh as the now-familiar Coral Cove P.D. squad car rolled up behind her rental.

Dylan exited the car and swooped in to take the laptop case from her. "Just wanted to make sure you made it over here okay."

"Did you think I'd get lost?" She wedged a hand on her hip. "How'd you know I was heading over here this morning anyway?"

"Uh, Alec gave me a call." The color heightened on his face as he shifted the case from one hand to the other.

"Do you have spies all over town keeping track of my every move, Chief?" She couldn't tell if the buzz at the base of her spine signaled annoyance or pleasure. She hadn't had anyone to look after her since her grandfather passed away, and truth be told, she'd been more of the caretaker than the other way around in that relationship.

"He just wanted to follow up to let me know you called. I asked him when you were coming by and happened to be in the area."

"Uh-huh." She lifted her chin toward the apartment building. "Let's not keep Mr. Computer Whiz waiting."

"Are you okay after last night?"

Did he mean the kiss or the thug? She glanced over her shoulder, noticing the lines creasing his brow. Must mean the thug.

"The guy never laid a hand on me, thanks to you."

"No thanks to me, he followed you to your motel in the first place."

"Working undercover with guys like that must've been one heckuva dangerous assignment. How'd your cover get blown?"

"I slipped up."

Then he zipped up. He'd closed the subject before it even got started. Noticing the square set of his shoulders and his compressed lips, Mia let it go.

He squeezed past her on the stairs. "He's on the second floor, corner unit."

He led the way and she followed, admiring the way his uniform fit his athletic frame. His rap on the door jolted her out of her dreaminess. No wonder people could anonymously leave dolls on her doorstep, chuck rocks at her and follow her home on a Harley without her noticing a thing. Dylan had been distracting her ever since she got to town.

A tall, wiry man opened the door. His eyebrows jumped when he saw both of them on his porch. "Wasn't expecting you, Dylan."

"I ran into Mia on the street. Do you remember Mia St. Regis? Mia, this is Alec Wright."

They shook hands and Alec squinted at her through his glasses. "You were ahead of me in school a few years, but I remember the St. Regis twins. Who didn't know the St. Regis twins?"

"I guess nobody." She nudged the laptop case hitched over Dylan's shoulder. "I hope you can help me recover my data."

Alec swung his door wide and pointed to a row of computer monitors and towers lining one wall of his small apartment. "If I can rescue your hard drive, I think we have a chance."

They crossed the room to the computer bank, and Mia pulled her laptop out of the case. "At least it didn't burn, but it got bounced around pretty good."

Alec booted up the computer, watched the error messages scroll down the blue screen and sucked in his cheek. "Yeah, there's some damage to the motherboard, but the hard drive might be salvageable."

"I hope so. I have…stuff I need on there."

"No backup?"

She held up her hands. "Guilty. I would occasionally drag important files and…and some pictures over to a flash drive, but I haven't done that in a few weeks."

"If I can recover anything, I'll put it on one of my computers." He tapped a monitor almost lovingly. "Then when you buy a new computer, I can transfer it over for you."

"That would be great." She turned to Dylan. "Is that big electronics store still by the outlet mall down the coast?"

"Still there. Are you going out there now?"

She narrowed her eyes. "Planning on a police escort?"

"No. I have a whole town to police."

Alec popped his head up from a cabinet he'd been rummaging in, clutching a cable. "I might have this ready by later this afternoon if you want to check back."

"That would be great."

They walked away from Alec's apartment building and Mia said, "You can follow me back to Main Street, if you're going back to the station. I'm popping in to see Linda Davis about the house."

"I am going back to the station, so don't think I'm following you around town."

Mia laughed, but the presence of Dylan's squad car behind her cast a comforting glow around her heart. What would it be like to have him to lean on always?

Dylan pulled his car into the small lot of the police station, and Mia cruised to the curb in front of Linda's Realty office. She waited next to her car until Dylan sauntered from the parking lot.

Mia hung the toes of her sandals off the edge of the curb. "Dinner later? Maybe?"

"Sure, if you don't feel like I'm smothering you."

A warm flush heated her cheeks more than the summer sun beating down her. "I don't feel smothered."

"I can't help feeling protective about you, Mimi."

"I know. You can't get past thinking of me as that dumb little girl."

"Oh, I think I'm past that."

The smolder in his blue eyes convinced her he *was* past thinking of her as a little girl.

Her feet moved toward him, his presence drawing her like a magnet. Someone burst out of the police station, and Mia jumped back.

Peter, his face red with purple blotches, stormed toward her, his fist shaking. "You bitch. You think you can toy with me? I'm going to kill you."

Chapter Seven

Mia staggered back as Dylan got between her and Peter's fist. Peter had always been snide but cool. She'd never seen this level of violence from him before.

He must've heard from the IRS.

"Whoa." Dylan slammed a hand into Peter's chest to halt his forward motion. "You need to back off."

Peter puffed out his chest in a belligerent stance. "Maybe *you'd* better back off. You don't know what you're dealing with. She's a black widow."

Yep, definitely the IRS.

Mia's gaze darted up and down the street. Like in any small town, people had come out of their shops or stopped on the sidewalk to watch the scene. Linda Davis hovered by her door, motioning to Mia to get inside her office.

"Sir, you need to go about your business. Whatever your issue with Mia, this isn't the time or the place."

"Do you want to know what she did? Or maybe she already told you." He snorted. "Oh, no, she'd want to keep that side of herself from you."

"Give it up, Peter. You're never going to get your hands on Columbella House."

"The witch snitched me off to the IRS." Peter ran an expensive sleeve across his sweating brow. "Don't even deny it."

"I don't know what you're talking about." Mia smoothed her cotton skirt over her thighs.

"It's not going to work, Mia. My attorney's working on getting that house turned over to me… something about fraud."

She flicked her fingers in the air. "Knock yourself out, Peter, but if you ever threaten to kill me again, or leave a voodoo doll for me or throw a rock at me, I'm going to take out a restraining order against you."

"This isn't over." He whipped around and marched down the street, with people scattering out of his way.

Mia dropped her shoulders, which had been hunched throughout Peter's tirade.

The tension must've been vibrating off her in waves because Dylan placed two hands on her shoulders and kneaded his thumbs into her tight muscle. "Are you going to try to tell me that guy isn't violent?"

Closing her eyes, she rolled her head back, wishing she was stretched out on a bed instead of standing in the middle of Main Street with a dissipating crowd throwing suspicious looks her way.

"I guess the IRS can turn the mildest of men into lions."

"Don't mess with me, Mia. Did you report him to the IRS?"

"Just doing my civic duty, Chief."

Linda Davis cleared her throat. "Come on in here and have a seat, Mia. I'll get you some water."

Dylan gave her shoulder a final squeeze. "Try to be careful. You have a way of driving men crazy."

"Really?" She batted her eyelashes. She'd done what she had to do to get Peter off her back. And she didn't regret it for one minute. It wasn't like she had to make up any stories. Peter had been cheating on his taxes, bragged about it, even. What did he expect?

"Go to your meeting. I'll call you later for dinner, or meet you at Alec's."

As Dylan walked away, Linda enfolded her in a perfumed hug. "Was that horrible man your ex-husband?"

Mia sighed and slumped into a chair across from Linda's desk. "Yeah. He's trying to get his hands on Columbella after he signed a prenup, fair and square."

"Mia, my dear, you have one complicated life."

Mia's gaze wandered to the window, where Dylan had stopped to talk to a couple of teenagers. He laughed and shoved his hair back from his face, and Mia's insides did a triple flip.

"Linda, you have no idea."

"No, I'M NOT DRIVING while holding my cell phone." Mia punched the button for Speaker and dropped her cell in her lap. "I'm on my way to Alec's place right now."

"Alec recovered your hard drive?"

"Yeah. He's good."

"I'm off duty, so I'll meet you over there."

Mia glanced in her rearview mirror for the hundredth time. "I don't have to worry about Peter. Despite his words, he's not a violent man."

Dylan snorted. "News flash. His actions and words in the street were violent. That makes him a violent man."

"Well, hopefully he'll be back in New York soon addressing his tax problems."

"You're playing with fire, Mia."

"I gotta go. I'm pulling into a drive-thru to get something to drink for the ride back."

"Drive carefully, and I'll see you at Alec's place."

Mia ordered a soda in the drive-thru and headed back up the coast to Coral Cove. When Alec had called her earlier to tell her that he'd been able to recover her hard drive, she'd wanted to kiss him through the phone.

So much of her future depended on the information on her computer, one piece of information in particular. Maybe that hard drive could even offer her some redemption.

Twenty minutes later, she pulled up to Alec's apartment building. She reached in the backseat and grabbed the new laptop. She'd let Alec set it up for her before he transferred the info.

Placing the computer on her lap, she sucked down the rest of her drink and waited for Dylan. She'd be happier if she knew that his attentiveness sprang from a desire to be with her rather than the conviction that he had to watch out for his sister's ditzy friend.

She didn't have to wait long. His squad car rolled up behind her, and he flashed his lights once.

She scrambled from her car, tucking the laptop under one arm. Gesturing at his uniform and car, she said, "I thought you were off duty."

"I am, but I came right from the station. Don't worry. I'll go home and change before we have dinner."

Worry? The uniform added a whole other layer of sex appeal to Dylan Reese—not that he needed any more layers of sex appeal.

Dylan took the laptop from her, and they climbed the stairs together. Alec showed no surprise at seeing Dylan this time, and invited them in.

He patted the computer. "I'm going to get this set up and start the transfer. Do you guys want something to drink?"

They both declined, and Alec got to work. Mia

hung over his shoulder while Dylan wandered around Alec's living room, tilting his head to read book and DVD titles.

Once Alec set up the new laptop, he hooked it up to one of his own computers. "This shouldn't take long."

Mia squinted at the green status bar, holding her breath as she tried to zero in on the file names flashing on the screen. She'd memorized the email she'd saved from Kylie Grant, but the phone number from that other email, the email from Kayla Rutherford, she needed that. Now more than ever.

"How's it going?" Dylan came up behind her and she jumped, which drew a puzzled glance from him.

Alec tapped a few more keys. "Almost done."

Dylan murmured in her ear, his warm breath brushing her lobe. "No more trouble from Peter today?"

"No. With any luck, he's heading back to New York to consult with a tax attorney."

"That's it." Alec unplugged the cable from her laptop, and moved the cursor to shut down the computer. "Do you want to check it out first?"

"Yes." She crowded him out of the way and opened her email. Alec had saved it—the email from Kayla almost glowed on the screen. She still had an opportunity to make everything right.

Mia threw her arms around a startled Alec.

"You're my new best friend. How much do I owe you?"

His face reddened. "That's okay. I did it as a favor to the chief. He got me out of a jam with my bike a few weeks ago."

"I can't accept gratuities, Alec." Dylan crossed his arms and winked at Mia. "Go ahead and charge her."

"Umm, well, okay. How about fifty dollars?"

"Fifty dollars for saving my life?" Mia dug her checkbook out of her bag and wrote him a check for considerably more.

Alec's eyes grew even larger behind his glasses when Mia handed him the check. "This is totally unnecessary."

"Keep it. Really, you have no idea how important those emails are to me."

He grinned and slipped the check into his pocket. "Okay, then. Glad I could help."

Mia packed up her new laptop, and Dylan insisted on carrying it out to her car for her, like she didn't have enough strength to hoist five pounds.

After he loaded it in her trunk, he leaned on her car door, blocking her from getting into the car. "Are you going to tell me why those emails are so important?"

Not yet. She didn't want to tell Dylan about Kayla, not until she'd had a chance to fix things. "Just work. Nothing to do with what's going on here, nothing to do with Peter."

His jaw visibly relaxed. "Promise me, no more funny business with Peter. Don't try to be the tough girl and deal with him on your own. He's dangerous, Mia. He threatened to kill you."

"I've never seen him like that before." She held up two fingers. "You have my word. If I see him lurking around anywhere, I'll call the police and get a restraining order."

He grabbed her fingers and pressed the tips to his lips. "I know you can handle yourself, but sometimes you don't take situations seriously enough."

"You know, sometimes you have to laugh just so you won't break down and cry." She slipped her hand from his and butted him off her car with her hip. "I'll buy you dinner in town tonight. Burgers and Brews?"

"It's a date."

"I'll meet you there, since we're coming from opposite directions."

He let her go without a protest. Of course, Mia could drive from the Sea View Motel into town on her own. He had to give her some space or she'd bolt back to New York faster than that husband of hers.

And he didn't want her bolting anywhere until they had some time to explore this chemistry between them. They'd never given themselves that chance before—or maybe he was just fooling himself, and she'd never felt anything special for him except brotherly affection.

He watched her car peel away from the curb, barely slowing down at the stop sign. She seemed to be in a big hurry to read over those recovered emails by herself. He didn't believe for one minute they were related to business. He could spot someone lying a mile away.

And Mia St. Regis was lying.

A FEW HOURS LATER, in a pair of jeans and a T-shirt instead of a uniform, Dylan shoved his hands in his pockets as he propped up the outside wall of Burgers and Brews. He'd already checked inside, but no Mia.

He couldn't help the way his palms had broken into a mild sweat and his blood had thumped a little harder through his veins when he didn't see her inside the restaurant.

Rocco Vick, the biker who'd accosted Mia, was on his way back to prison, but Rocco didn't leave that doll. Dylan hadn't gotten verification from anyone that Peter Casellas had left Coral Cove. Dylan had firsthand knowledge of too many murders committed by jealous lovers or duped business partners. When emotions ran high, people committed unspeakable acts.

People did crazy things. Look at Mia. She'd figured tempting her sister with another man while Marissa was already engaged to marry Tyler Davis amounted to fun and games. Now she hadn't seen her sister since that practical joke.

Dylan hadn't realized until Mia came back to town that Marissa had disappeared off the face of the earth, except for a few postcards.

Did Mia still have the postcards?

"You could've grabbed a table inside." Mia strode down the sidewalk with a bounce to her step. "Sorry I'm late."

"Ten minutes. That doesn't count." He pushed open the door for her, and the waves of noise washed over them, sucking them into the lights and action.

As the hostess led them to their table, several people waved to him and called out a greeting, their eyes shifting to Mia. She waved back, oblivious to the fact that their hospitality didn't include her, or knowing full well it didn't and enjoying the joke on them.

Dylan yanked out Mia's chair, and the hostess dropped two plastic menus on their table before scurrying away to seat more people jammed at the entrance.

Mia's gaze swept the dining room. "It's that last desperate two weeks of summer before the kids go back to school, people come back from vacations and the routine kicks in again."

Dylan toyed with the menu, running his thumb along the edge, as he studied the variety of beers and microbrews. "I would've thought you'd want to make your return once everyone got back to their routine."

She shook out her menu and tapped it on the table. "Oh, I don't know. There's something special about this time of year in Coral Cove."

"Admit it." He nudged her. "You missed the place."

"Like you must've missed it to come back—as chief, no less."

"I had my reasons." Reasons he preferred not to divulge right now...or ever.

"Me, too." She slid a sly look his way over the top of her menu. "I had my reasons."

They both ordered burgers with a cone of fries to share, while Dylan added a beer and Mia stuck with iced tea. He tapped her glass with a fork. "No margaritas tonight?"

Shaking her head, she dumped a packet of artificial sweetener into her tea. "I figure if I hadn't been tipsy last night, I never would've opened the door to...what's-his-name."

"Rocco."

"Yeah, Rocco. Especially once he told me his name was Rocco."

"I have another name for you—Peter. Have you gotten word that he's left town yet?"

"He wouldn't tell me, would he?"

"Maybe his tax troubles will be enough to keep him busy and out of your hair."

"My exact thought when I reported him to the IRS."

Dylan studied Mia's beautiful face with one

abrasion and one scratch on her chin as he sipped his beer through the foam. "I wouldn't want to be your enemy."

"That—" she shook her napkin into her lap as the waitress delivered their burgers in baskets "—would never happen."

"Whew. Not that I don't always pay my taxes."

"I have ways of finding out." She squeezed a stream of ketchup onto a plate and swept a French fry through the glop.

"Speaking of investigations, sort of. Do you still have those postcards Marissa sent you from around the globe?"

The fingers pinching the fry froze halfway to her mouth and a drop of ketchup dribbled on the table. "I have them with me. Do you want to see them?"

"Yeah, since Matt's too busy getting his job back with the LAPD, I can at least look into it." He sliced his burger in half and stuffed an onion back inside the bun. "Drop them off at the station."

Chewing, she crumpled the napkin against her mouth. "I have them with me, on me, in my bag."

He raised his brows. She carried the postcards with her? She must really have a guilt complex about her twin. If those emails she'd been so secretive about concerned Marissa, maybe Mia would confide in him about them now that he'd volunteered to look into her sister's disappearance.

Mia scrubbed her hands with the napkin and dipped into the big bag she'd been slinging along

with her ever since her purse got scorched in the
wreck. She waved a handful of cards under his
nose before dropping them on top of the tablecloth.

"Don't get grease on them."

He wiped his own hands and picked up the first
card by the corner. A pretty coastal scene with
Cote-d'Azur in yellow scrawl in the corner. He
flipped it over. *Hey, Mimi. All is well. Enjoying
life with Raoul on the French Riviera. Hope you
don't mind that I stole him.*

"That's the first one I received." She tapped the
rest of the pile. "They're in order."

Dylan drew his brows over his nose. With all the
social networking sites, email and text messaging,
he didn't realize people even sent postcards from
abroad anymore. Of course, these started a while
ago, when Marissa first took off.

"When did you get the last one?"

"Last summer." Mia shuffled to the bottom of
the pile and slid out a card from Spain. The message on the back was as innocuous and generic as
the first, more so.

"Have you gotten one every summer since she
took off?"

"Just about. Sh-she missed a few summers."

"Never any return addresses or hotel names? Is
she still with Raoul?"

Mia shrugged. "Nothing. It's as if she doesn't
want me to find her, or..."

"Or you believe Kylie Grant." He stacked the

cards in a neat pile. "Who would be sending these cards and why?"

She sat forward and planted her elbows on the table. "Maybe it's Raoul. Maybe he killed her and he's living off her money."

Dylan eyed Mia's knife balanced across her plate, dripping bloodred ketchup. "Was Raoul that kind of guy?"

"You're asking me?" She slurped a noisy gulp of tea through her straw. "I didn't know Peter was the type of guy to stick pins in dolls. What do I know about men?"

If she didn't know she was turning him on even sitting here talking about murder and mayhem with a dribble of ketchup at the corner of her luscious mouth, she knew nothing.

Leaving her question for another time, he dabbed his fingertip at the ketchup on her face. "If your New York cronies could see you now."

Her eyes glazed over for a second, and then she dropped her sloppy burger in the basket. "This is serious, Dylan."

"Mia St. Regis. How the hell are you?"

Mia's eyes widened as they stared past Dylan's shoulder, and he twisted his head to the side to see the owner of the booming voice.

Charlie Vega, one of the biggest contractors in Coral Cove, descended on their table, his face split into a wide grin. "Hey, Chief."

"Charlie." Dylan shook his hand, but Mia looked like a zombie had just approached them.

Charlie extended his beefy hand to Mia, and she placed her slightly trembling fingers in his paw. "H-hello, Charlie."

"I hope you're here to make some sense of Columbella House. Keep Vega Construction in mind whether you're going to restore it or tear it down and rebuild." He winked.

"I will, yeah, absolutely."

Charlie's brow creased but he nodded. "Okay, then. Wife's waiting for me outside. See you around, Chief. Great to see a St. Regis twin in town."

Charlie shouldered his way through the clutch of people hovering around the hostess stand, while Mia sat stiffly in her chair, not turning around.

"What was that all about?" He tilted his chin toward the front door. "Do you have a problem with Charlie Vega?"

"Charlie? N-no."

"You could've fooled me. Charlie noticed, too."

She pushed her basket to the middle of the table. "That's because Charlie probably doesn't realize that I know."

"Know what?" Dylan gripped the edge of the table. Mia had returned to town loaded with bombshells. He didn't know what to expect from her next.

She glanced over her shoulder as if expecting

Charlie to be listening in. Then she cupped a hand around her mouth and whispered, "He slept with Marissa."

Dylan's fingers slipped from the table and he dropped back in his seat. "Is that all? Marissa slept with a lot of guys."

"Not you." Her eyes widened and her face paled. "Not you?"

Throwing his head back, he laughed at the ceiling. "God, no."

She sniffed. "Not good enough for you."

"Which is it?" He lifted one eyebrow. "You hope I didn't sleep with your sister, and then you're offended I didn't want to?"

"You could've just said no without the wild laughter."

"Excuse my wild laughter. It's just that Marissa shared all your good looks and none of your wit and charm."

"Apparently, she didn't share my deviousness either." She held up her hand at his protest. "Back to Charlie. Don't forget, he has a good ten years on us. He slept with Marissa when she was only sixteen, and he was probably close to twenty-six."

"That's creepy when you put it that way."

"That's statutory rape, no matter how willing she was at the time."

"Do you want me to arrest him now?"

"Don't be silly. Just creeps me out to see him."

"That's a long time ago now. I don't think he's running around seducing teenage girls anymore."

"Hope not." She patted the front pocket of her jeans. "Message."

She pulled out her cell phone and frowned at the display, biting her lip.

"What is it?"

"Peter."

Dylan set his jaw. He'd had about enough of this guy. "I hope he's sending that message from an airplane."

"Nope." She dropped the phone in the middle of the table. "He's at Columbella."

"You're kidding. Does he intend to squat there until you sign it over to him?"

"He wants me to meet him there."

"No way."

"He said he has some information that might change my mind."

"Forget it, Mia."

"What if you and your—" her gaze dropped to the gun bag clipped around his waist "—weapon come with me?"

He waved to the waitress. "Is there anything he can tell you at this point to make you change your mind?"

"No, but if he has some information, possibly about Marissa, I want to hear it."

"He doesn't have anything. He's playing you."

Dylan asked the waitress for the check, and she slapped it down on the table.

Mia grabbed it first. "Peter knows I've been looking for my sister. Maybe he's been holding on to the information."

"Maybe he's desperate."

"Then I need to know that, too." She dropped some bills on the table and anchored them with the ketchup bottle. "Come with me, Chief."

"I sure as hell am not going to let you go out there by yourself."

"What are we waiting for?" She punched a response into her phone and pushed back from the table.

Ten minutes later and against his better judgment, Dylan wheeled his truck on to the Coast Highway, Mia buzzing with excitement next to him.

"Before Peter got antagonistic, he was helping me find Marissa. Who knows? Maybe he turned up something and kept it to himself as ammunition."

Clamping a hand on her bouncing knee, he said, "Peter just wants another crack at you. That's all. But he's going to have to try to get through me first."

The idea of Peter getting through Dylan or around Dylan or over Dylan brought a smile to her lips. She just wanted to see the look on Peter's face when she showed up with her own personal lawman.

Dylan aimed his truck toward the Coral Cove Drive exit. As they rumbled down the street, his headlights picked out a car on the lookout point. Peter could've easily parked there and walked to the front of the house where he wanted to meet her.

Dylan parked his truck. "You really want to do this?"

"Of course. Do you have a flashlight?"

"In the trunk, but I'll leave my headlights on, too." Their glow illuminated the overgrown yard in the front. "I don't see him."

"Maybe he's taking in the lovely view before he goes home." Mia scrambled out of the trunk and hopped to the ground.

Dylan emerged from the trunk, gripping a flashlight. "Casellas?"

"Shh. I wanted to spring you on him."

"You're not springing anything on anybody. The guy is dangerous."

Their footsteps crunched on the sidewalk as they crossed to the front gate of Columbella. Dylan swept the beam of his flashlight across the tangled shrubbery and tracked across the porch. Empty.

"Peter?" Mia pushed open the front gate, which creaked with rust and sand. "I'm here with Chief Reese. Tell me what you got."

Her only answer came from the waves beating against the rocks below.

"Maybe he's still in his car?"

They walked back up the sidewalk toward the

lookout point where a car sat in darkness. A chill snaked up Mia's spine and she tucked in closer to Dylan as he approached the car.

Dylan leaned forward, cupping a hand over his eyes as he peered into the car window.

Mia hooked a finger in his belt loop. "See anything?"

"Bags in the backseat."

"That's a good sign."

Dylan straightened up and scanned the lookout area. "Where is he?"

"Maybe he's waiting inside the house."

"Didn't the text message ask you to meet him out front?"

"It did." Mia fished in the pocket of her sweater for the phone and reread Peter's message.

"Call him." Dylan scuffed to the front of the car where it pointed toward the ocean and unzipped his gun bag. "I don't like this."

"Y-you think it's an ambush?" She fumbled with the buttons on her phone.

"Something's not right."

"Maybe he saw you coming and got scared off." She held the phone away from her ear. "It's ringing."

Dylan cocked his head. "Listen."

Amid the waves crashing on the rocks and the hollow boom from the tunnel carved into those rocks, came the tinny sound of a ringing phone.

Mia spun around toward the car. "Is it in his car?"

"No." Dylan took two steps closer to the low metal barrier around the edge of the overlook. He squatted to his haunches, his brows colliding over his nose. "Dial again."

With a shaky finger, Mia punched the button to redial. The phone rang again, the ocean breeze snatching the sound so that it seemed to surround her.

Dylan dropped to his knees, skimming the light from his flashlight along the ledge of rock over the barrier. His arm shot out. "It's there, just below the ledge on the rocks. I can see the light from it."

He flattened to his belly and army-crawled toward the edge.

The knots that had been forming in Mia's stomach the minute she heard Peter's disembodied phone ringing, cinched tighter. "Be careful."

Dylan scooted forward another few inches and then swore.

Clutching her sweater around her trembling body, Mia shuffled to the edge of the precipice. "What is it, Dylan?"

Her gaze followed the beam of his light as it tripped down the vicious rocks. White foam rushed in and swirled around the rocks and something else…a body.

Chapter Eight

The fist Mia shoved into her mouth couldn't stop the scream barreling up her throat. She swayed forward and Dylan caught her around the waist.

"Call 911. I'm heading down there."

She fumbled for her phone. "I'm coming with you."

While she babbled on the phone, Dylan grabbed her hand and pulled her along the road to the other side of the house and the path that led down to the beach.

Shoving the phone in her pocket, she panted, trying to force air into her lungs. "They're on their way."

They hit the sandy beach, and Mia kicked off her sandals to keep up with Dylan striding toward the cave. They'd have to skirt the cave near the water to get to the other side where the body lay.

Peter? Was it Peter?

Dylan balanced a foot on the first rock. "Stay here and wait for the emergency response team."

"I told them exactly where…" She flapped her arms. "They don't need me to guide them, and I don't want to stand on this beach alone."

"Okay, follow me." He grabbed her hand again and hopped from rock to rock around the cave, pulling her along with him as the spray from the waves dampened their clothing.

They reached the other side and headed for the body crumpled on the rocks.

Mia gulped. She recognized the blue jacket. Now that Peter's body lay only feet away from her, she froze. She folded her arms, tucking her hands against her sides. "You go ahead."

With her teeth chattering, she watched Dylan forge a path across the rocks, the light from the flashlight bouncing ahead of him. He seemed to melt into the darkness, and panic washed over Mia until she spotted his light again as he crouched near the body.

Sirens blared in the distance, and Mia licked her lips, tasting the salt from the sea. Or was it the salt from her tears?

Had Peter committed suicide? Was that what he wanted to show her? Did he want to heap more guilt on her head?

Dylan called over his shoulder, "It's Peter."

Mia had already known that, but the confirmation carried by Dylan's words turned her legs to spaghetti and she sank onto the wet sand.

The sirens came to a stop and the glow from the

red lights above splashed the water and rocks. A voice boomed over a loudspeaker. "Chief Reese, is that you down there?"

Dylan pushed to his feet and waved his arms over his head. He tromped back to her and scooped her up in his arms. "Are you okay?"

"Peter's dead."

"Died from the fall. Looks like he broke his neck."

Gasping, she buried her head in the hollow between Dylan's shoulder and neck. He squeezed her tighter, their wet clothes meshing together.

He carried her back around the cave and across the sand as her legs beat limply against his thighs. He set her down next to her sandals. "Can you climb back up?"

"Yes." She cleared her throat. "Yes."

She ascended the rocks toward the house, while Dylan acted as a buffer behind her, catching her each time she slipped, planting a steadying hand against the small of her back.

When they reached the top, the entire Coral Cove police and fire departments swarmed toward them, peppering them with questions.

"Who is it?"

"Did you see him fall?"

"Is he dead?"

Dylan draped an arm around her shoulders and guided her toward his truck. "Ms. St. Regis needs to warm up. You can ask her any questions in my truck."

He settled her in the passenger seat after starting the engine of the truck and cranking on the heat. He pulled a sweatshirt from the backseat and dropped it into her lap. "Warm up, and tell Lieutenant Trammell everything that happened from the minute you got that text message from Peter."

She nodded, shrugged out of her wet sweater and pulled Dylan's sweatshirt over her head. Not wanting to get the sweatshirt wet and anxious to shed the drenched blouse sticking to her skin, she shimmied out of the blouse beneath the sweatshirt.

Pressing her nose to the window, she saw Dylan open Peter's car and duck inside. He must've taken the keys from Peter's pocket. She shivered and snuggled further into the bulky sweatshirt.

A minute later, a dark shape cut off her view of Dylan, and Clark Trammell tapped on the window. She buzzed it down.

"Can I ask you a few questions, Mia—Ms. St. Regis?"

"Mia's fine."

Trammell took her through her actions after receiving Peter's message at dinner. "Can I see your phone, please?"

She felt the front pocket of her jeans, and then dragged her sweater up from the floor. She plucked the cell phone out of the sweater pocket and dropped it into Trammell's hand. "It's kind of damp."

He jabbed a button. "Still works. Can you show me Mr. Casellas's message?"

Her eyes narrowed as she took her phone back from Trammell. The lieutenant would be looking at her as the prime suspect if she hadn't been with the chief. She pulled up Peter's text and thrust the phone back at Trammell.

Trammell squinted at the message and adjusted his cap, pushing it back on his head. "Didn't you have an altercation with your husband in the street today?"

"Altercation?" Her gaze shifted past Tramell to Dylan, reenacting his discovery of Peter's cell phone. Her eyelid twitched. Did Dylan's officers suspect him, too? He'd been hanging out with her too much since her return to town.

Tramell cleared his throat.

Mia blinked. "Ex-husband. I wouldn't call it an altercation."

"Thought you two were still married. That doesn't make you a divorcée, Ms. St. Regis. That makes you a widow."

She chewed her bottom lip. What happened to calling her *Mia?* "The divorce was all but a done deal. Peter just had to sign some papers."

"Exactly."

She jumped beneath Dylan's sweatshirt, and a

shiver rippled over her skin. Exactly what? Had she just implicated herself in something?

Trammell scratched his chin, trying to look innocent or bumbling or something. Didn't work.

"Why would you go to meet your soon-to-be ex, in the middle of the night, at a deserted house?"

"He said he had some information for me. I believed him." She shrugged. "Besides, Dyl—Chief Reese was coming with me."

Dylan jogged back to the car, his face joining Trammell's at the open window. She preferred his.

"Are you warming up in here?"

"Yes. What's going on?"

"A few of the officers went down to the body. We checked out Peter's car, and we retrieved his cell phone."

She hugged the sweatshirt around her torso. "What does it look like? Did he jump? Did he fall?"

"Was he pushed?"

Trammell's words socked her in the gut, even though he'd been hinting around this conclusion for the past ten minutes.

Either Dylan didn't catch his lieutenant's implication or he didn't care because he simply lifted a shoulder. "No way to tell right now. He didn't leave any suicide note. There's no sign of a scuffle at the drop-off. There's no new erosion or crumbling of the rock that would point to a fall. We'll have to see what the coroner says. Peter might have some evidence on his body—maybe a suicide note in his pocket, an injury in addition to the fall, skin beneath his fingernails if he scratched someone on his way over."

Was Trammell studying her face with new interest? She had to sit on her hands so she wouldn't be tempted to shove her hair back from her face and show him her unmarred skin, except for those injuries on her chin.

Dylan smacked him on the back. "I'm leaving this possible crime scene in your capable hands, Lieutenant, since I'm, uh…personally involved."

"You got it, Chief. Thanks for your cooperation, Mia."

Oh, now it was back to "Mia"?

When Trammell turned and loped back to the possible crime scene, Mia powered up the window. She held her breath as Dylan climbed into the truck.

He snapped on his seat belt and squeezed her knee beneath the sweatshirt. "Are you okay?"

"Your lieutenant thinks I had something to do with Peter's death."

"He wouldn't be a good cop if he didn't." He pulled away from the curb, waving out his window to his officers still combing the lookout. "And Clark's a good cop."

"A-am I, are we, in trouble?"

"You and I are innocent and have nothing to hide. Depending on how closely the coroner sets the time of death, we also have an alibi. Lots of people saw us at Burgers and Brews. Don't worry."

She covered her eyes, burning with tears, with one hand and sniffed. "I can't believe Peter would kill himself over an impending investigation by the IRS."

"Then he probably didn't. If it is suicide, I'm sure he had more reasons than an IRS investigation."

"If I'm responsible for Peter's death..."

Dylan cinched her wrist. "Stop. Even if he did kill himself over his tax issues, it's not your fault."

"First Marissa, now Peter and you're next."

The truck lurched to a stop at the stop sign at the entrance to the Coast Highway. "What does that mean?"

"Those cops back there were suspicious, suspicious of me and then suspicious of you—guilt by association. What if you lose your job over this, or your reputation? The people of Coral Cove love Chief Reese, but not for long if he continues to keep company with the town pariah."

He snorted as he wheeled onto the highway. "Their idolization of Chief Reese has nothing to do with me and everything to do with my father. They don't know Chief Reese as well as they think they do."

She peeked at him through her fingers, the oncoming headlights illuminating the sharp planes of his face, the light spilling onto the tattoo stamped across his arm.

Did she know Chief Reese as well as she thought she did? Obviously, she wasn't the only one in this car with secrets. Maybe one of these days if she spilled hers, he'd spill his.

He'd never wanted to work for the Coral Cove P.D., and yet here he was. Something must've driven him back. Would he ever confide in her? Still, she had no intention of blowing into town and mucking up the place Dylan had carved for himself here.

"Was that normal for your department to continue the investigation without you?"

"Absolutely. I discovered the body. I'd gone there to meet the victim."

"We don't know yet if he's a victim."

"Could just be the victim of an accident, still a victim."

Tossing her cell phone between her two hands, she sighed. "I suppose I should notify Peter's sister. She's his closest relative."

"Were you close to her?"

"Met her once."

"If you'd like, the P.D. can notify her."

She clasped the phone in her hands. "That's kind of cold, isn't it? She doesn't know half the stuff Peter was trying to pull. She knew ours wasn't a real marriage, but never got involved."

"There's no need for you to tell her."

"Not unless Lieutenant Trammell arrests me for Peter's murder."

"I was there as a witness. Nobody's going to arrest you."

"Maybe they'll arrest you, too."

"Just stop running around saying you're to blame for Peter's death."

"Ah-ha!" She smacked her knees. "You *are* worried."

"I think you need to get back to your motel, have a warm bath and a glass of wine."

"I'm at the Sea View, remember? Not exactly the lap of luxury."

She sealed her lips for the rest of the ride back to her car parked outside Burgers and Brews. The night had turned ugly. Peter's death had caused a tumult of emotions to course through her body, but she didn't want to dump any more on Dylan.

She'd process them on her own—maybe in the chipped tub of her motel room clutching a plastic cup of cheap wine from the convenience store next to the Sea View.

Dylan pulled in behind her car, and she turned to him. "I'm sorry things turned out like they did."

"Save your apology." He shoved open his door. "You're not getting rid of me yet. I'm going to follow you back to the motel."

"That's completely unnecessary—" she held up her hand as he opened his mouth "—but totally appreciated."

The headlights of Dylan's truck tagged her all

the way back to the Sea View. He parked on the street and then met her by the office.

"I'm going to see you all the way to your door and listen while you lock it."

"I'm not the one who wound up broken on the rocks tonight."

"No, but you got a text message before Peter took the plunge. Who knows? Maybe someone else sent that text from Peter's phone."

An icy finger traced a line down her back, and she hunched her shoulders. "Now you're being paranoid. Why would someone want to kill Peter *and* me?"

"I don't know, Mia, but you've been involved in a lot of crazy stuff since you got back."

"Maybe Peter generated all that crazy stuff and couldn't live with himself anymore. Maybe that's why he sent me the message."

"We can stand here and speculate all night, but we don't have proof of anything yet." He snagged the key from her hand and shoved it into the lock. "And it doesn't lessen my worry for you, so get a good night's sleep and we'll see in a few days what the coroner has to say about Peter."

She leaned against the doorjamb, eyes downcast. If he really wanted to see to her safety, why didn't he come in? Why didn't he join her in that chipped tub?

His knuckles skimmed her cheek. "Are you all

right? I know you and Peter used to be friends, no matter what happened at the end."

Another rush of guilt heated her cheeks. Dylan had assumed she was mourning her old friend, probably not even out of the coroner's van yet, and instead she was imagining what it would feel like to run her hands over Dylan's wet, naked body.

She shook her head. "He changed so much. I don't know what to think. I'm sad, I'm angry, I'm confused."

"Just don't say *guilty* again." He threaded his fingers through her hair. As he cupped the back of her head, he dipped for a quick kiss. "We'll talk more tomorrow."

Talk? She wanted more than talk from him. She ached to be in his arms, and if she threw herself there he wouldn't let her down. But she had the stench of death on her. She didn't blame him if he wanted far, far away.

"I'm glad you were with me tonight, Dylan."

"Me, too."

Sounded like dismissal to her. She stepped backward into the cold, lonely room and snapped the door shut. She clicked the deadbolt in place and then, feeling Dylan's presence on the other side of the door, she laid her cheek on the scarred wood.

She couldn't bring her brand of bad luck to Dylan. She wouldn't do it.

She pushed off the door and slipped out of her sandals. Padding to the mini fridge, she swept the remote control from the console and aimed it at the TV. She'd stored a couple of bottles of water in the fridge earlier, but no cheap wine.

Tugging at the sleeve of her sweatshirt, she pulled it up. *Dylan's sweatshirt.* She yanked it off her body. She could probably still catch him and give herself a good excuse to see him one more time.

Halfway to the door, she realized she didn't have a top on. She ran back to her gaping suitcase in the corner and grabbed a T-shirt and then stumbled back to the door.

She threw it open and charged outside. "Dylan?"

The figure materialized from the shadows. Mia tripped to a stop, clutching the sweatshirt to her chest.

When the intruder took another step forward, the lights from the courtyard illuminated the scene.

Mia's eyes widened and she gasped. "It's you, isn't it?"

Chapter Nine

Dylan's eyes narrowed as he watched the hooded figure exit the battered car that had been parked down the road when he and Mia had arrived. He hadn't noticed anyone in the car then.

His senses clicked into focus and he slid out of the car. If Rocco Vick could track down Mia, maybe others from the Lords could, too. He crept past the silent office and edged into the courtyard. The person with the hood was parked in the center of the courtyard, facing Mia, whose mouth gaped open.

That was all he needed.

He prowled across the cement, his gun drawn and positioned in front of him. "Stop right there."

Two faces turned toward him, lit up by the overhead lights. Two almost identical faces. He blinked and a swirl of confusion claimed his brain.

Mia gave a cry and stepped in front of the other woman. "Dylan, put that away. She's no threat."

Still grasping his weapon, Dylan dropped his

hand to his side, but continued forward. "Are you okay, Mia? Who is this?"

The woman, girl, stepped out from behind Mia and peeled the hood from her head. Dark hair, the light highlighting chestnut strands, tumbled around her face—a perfect face with high cheekbones, wide-set eyes and full lips.

Dylan took a step back. How many secrets did the woman have?

"I-is this your daughter, Mia?"

"Daughter? No, no. This is my niece. This is Marissa's daughter."

Of course. This girl was a teenager. He knew Mia had never been pregnant in high school, but Marissa?

He blew out a breath and shoved his gun back into his bag. "I'm sorry. It's just..." He waved his arms around. "What are you doing out here?"

"She just arrived." Mia turned uncertainly toward the girl, who hadn't uttered one word. "C-can we... Do you want to come inside?"

The girl nodded, and Mia led the way with Dylan hot on their heels. Niece or not, he didn't trust this silent girl with the petulant pout.

They crowded into Mia's small room, the TV blaring some reality show.

Mia's hands fluttered. "Sit."

Then she grabbed the remote and muted the TV, dropping to the bed as if her legs couldn't support her anymore.

Dylan folded his arms over his chest and leaned against the door, his gaze tracking back and forth between aunt and niece. The air between them crackled with tension and unasked questions, unsaid words.

As the outsider, he might as well defuse the situation...or make it worse. He pushed off the door and stepped between them. "I'm Dylan Reese."

The girl met his eyes with a fiery gaze, and gave him a strong handshake. "I know—the police chief."

Mia sucked in a breath behind him. "How did you know that?"

Still without giving her own name, Mia's niece bobbed to the side to make eye contact with Mia. "I've been here a few days."

"You have? How did you know I was here?"

The girl tossed back her long hair. "I found out. It was easy."

"I was going to contact you." Mia's tongue darted out of her mouth and swept across her lips. "I wanted to wait until I got here, and then my computer got damaged."

This did not sound right. Dylan reached around the girl and drew up a chair, almost touching the back of her knees. He pressed an index finger on top of her shoulder. "You, sit down."

Then he crossed to the mini fridge and swept out the remaining bottles of water and handed them around. He joined Mia on the bed. Her niece had rattled her somehow, and he didn't plan on letting Mia sit over here on her own taking the heat from some teenager.

"Okay, why don't we start from the top?" He tipped his water bottle toward the teen. "What's your name?"

"Kayla Rutherford."

"Rutherford?"

"My *adopted* name." Her gaze darted toward Mia, and a scowl marred her pretty features.

Mia flinched beside him.

He nudged a knuckle beneath Mia's chin and turned her head toward him. "Why didn't you know that Kayla was here or coming here?"

She swallowed and folded her hands in her lap. "Kayla and I have never met before tonight."

"Ah." That explained the awkwardness. "But you knew of her existence?"

"She had emailed me a few weeks ago." Mia tilted her chin and stared into Kayla's eyes. "That's the first I knew of Marissa having a daughter."

Kayla snorted, folded her arms and turned her head.

"Young lady—" Dylan suddenly felt like his dad "—if your aunt told you she didn't know of your existence, she's telling the truth."

Kayla whipped her head back so fast, her hood dropped to her shoulders. "How do you not know your twin sister is pregnant? Lame."

"I didn't want to put all this junk in an email,

Kayla." Mia bounced forward on the bed until her feet braced against the floor. "Your mother studied abroad her junior year of high school. Our grandparents must've hidden her pregnancy that way, and nobody bothered to tell me. By the time Marissa came home—" Mia flattened a hand against her belly "—she'd already given birth."

Dylan raised his hand. "I can verify that. Marissa did go away that school year. Don't you think everyone in this small town would've talked about a pregnant teen if she'd been living here?"

A fat tear rolled down Kayla's cheek. "She didn't even tell her own sister, her twin?"

When the tear dripped to Kayla's chin, Mia launched off the bed and crouched next to her niece. "I feel the same way. Your initial email stunned me."

The girl swiped at her face with the back of her hand. "Is that why you waited so long to meet me?"

Mia fell back on her bottom, wrapping her arms around her legs and rocking. "Two weeks? You send me an email announcing you're my long-lost niece, and you expect contact faster than two weeks?"

"I expected… I expected…" Kayla shook her head and rubbed her nose with the heel of her hand.

Mia crossed her legs and grasped Kayla's knees. "I know. You expect everything right now."

"My father's here."

This was gonna be good. Dylan hunched forward. Did Mia know who Kayla's father was?

"You've contacted him?"

Yep, she knew.

"No. I just found out where he was and followed him around for a few hours."

Had she been following Mia around, too? "Who's your father?"

Mia twisted her head over her shoulder. "It's Charlie Vega."

That made sense after the way Mia reacted to him tonight at dinner. "Does he know?"

"I—I haven't told him yet."

"I'll come with you when you tell him." Mia's hand hovered above Kayla's knee as if to pat her and then dropped it in her own lap.

"That's okay. I'm going to do it myself."

How long had this girl been wandering around town and why the attitude? "Where do you live and how'd you get here? Where are you staying in Coral Cove?"

She widened heavily lined eyes. "You sound like a cop."

"We already established that. You got any answers?"

"I live in Arizona. My parents let me take a road trip with some friends after I graduated from high school. I didn't have to twist my friends' arms to come out to the beach in California."

"Where are you staying?" Mia worried her bottom lip, looking like a concerned aunt.

Kayla waved one arm toward the window. "We're camping at that campsite down the coast. I've been taking the car or hitching a ride to get into town."

Mia sucked in a breath and jerked her head up. "You shouldn't be hitchhiking. We've had some murders recently in Coral Cove."

"Well, I have the car now." The girl scrambled out of the chair. "And I have to get back before the campsite closes."

"I'll walk you out." Dylan pushed up from the bed.

Mia hopped to her feet. "Me, too."

Kayla shrugged and yanked up her hood, but not before Dylan saw a pink blush creep onto her cheeks beneath the makeup.

When they reached the car on the street, Mia enfolded Kayla in a hug and slipped a piece of paper in her pocket. "That's my cell phone number. Call me anytime, and maybe—" she glanced at Dylan "—maybe Chief Reese and I can buy you dinner tomorrow night?"

"Maybe." She slipped into the car and cruised away from the curb.

Mia expelled a long sigh. "Wow."

"Why does she have a chip on her shoulder? I mean, other than the fact that she's a teenager." Dylan steered Mia back to her room.

"We exchanged a couple of emails. She'd been trying to locate Marissa—like everyone else. Failing that, she tracked me down. After her initial introduction she went off on me for trying to *disown her*—her words."

"I assume she was adopted through the normal channels and not left in a basket on the side of the road?"

Mia plucked a couple of dried flowers from the bougainvillea in the courtyard. "From what I could gather, she had a nice, middle-class upbringing."

"So what's her problem?"

"Ah, the old St. Regis curse." She rolled her eyes at him and tossed the flowers into the air. "Kayla not only found her birth mother, she found out about her birth mother's family and all the wealth and power."

"And the crazy stuff?" He grabbed her key and shoved it into the lock. "Did she find out about all the crazy stuff, too?"

"That never seems to matter once they discover the money and property."

Dylan froze, his hand still gripping the key and door handle. "Kayla knows about the St. Regis money and...Columbella House?"

"Yeah, maybe she has a future as a research assistant or a librarian. She'd done her homework before contacting me."

He pushed open the door and propped up the doorjamb as Mia squeezed past him, her sweet scent tickling his nostrils. "Are you going to verify her identity?"

Laughing, Mia poked him in the chest. "You thought she was my daughter. Is there any doubt she's a St. Regis? She looks just like us at that age, except she got Charlie's height."

His face burned. For a minute, he'd forgotten the strong family resemblance. "So she's interested in getting her hands on the St. Regis riches?"

"What makes you say that?"

He poked her back in the chest. "She brought it up, didn't she? She's disgruntled that you've been holding out on her."

"Sort of." Mia backed up a few steps and took a swig of water from the bottle she'd left on the nightstand. "What's your point?"

"You know my point. She's been in town for a while. She's had an opportunity to leave that doll at your door, maybe throw a rock at you."

Mia choked on the water, spewing it down the front of his sweatshirt, which she'd pulled on outside. "You're kidding."

"No."

"Do you think she had something to do with Peter's death, too?"

"You don't think Peter committed suicide?" He studied her as several different emotions struggled for dominance on her face. Confusion won.

"I don't know, but you seem to be laying all the

sins of Coral Cove at Kayla's feet. I thought I'd throw one more on the pile."

He narrowed his eyes. "You're not going to go all goo-goo-ga-ga sentimental about Marissa's daughter and give her Columbella House, are you?"

She tossed back her hair. "When have you known me to go goo-goo-ga-ga?"

"You have a point." Those tears she'd shed for Peter had probably been the first bout of waterworks he'd ever witnessed from her.

"Of course," she added, peeling a corner of the label from the water bottle, "I am going to give her something."

"That makes sense. What do you think Charlie's going to make of having a teenage daughter? More to the point, what's his wife going to think?"

"I don't know. Charlie's an easygoing guy, and what's his wife going to say? His fling with my sister happened seventeen years ago."

"When he was twenty-six."

"Not going to look good, but that girl is hell-bent on making up for lost time."

He reached out and caught her around the waist. "Be careful. Make your decision about Columbella and get out of town."

Her body stiffened beneath his hands and she blinked her eyes rapidly. Damn. He hadn't meant it to come out like that.

"There's too much turmoil surrounding that house, and your long-lost niece has just added to it."

She shrugged out of his grasp and tossed the empty water bottle into the small trash can across the room. It hit the rim and bounced onto the floor. "Don't worry. I'll make my decision and then I'm outta this dump."

"Mia—"

"You know what I don't get?" She spun around, her arms clenched over her chest, her eyes bright. "What the hell are you doing back here? When you were growing up, you swore you wanted big city lights and big city crime. You never wanted to be another Chief Reese of Coral Cove. I guess it was just easier, huh?"

"I…"

She gripped his sweatshirt and with flushed cheeks in her sexy black bra, she tossed it at him.

He made a grab for it, but it fell in a puddle at his feet. He bent over, scooped it up and headed for the door. "Yeah, it was just easier."

MIA PUNCHED HER PILLOW. It wasn't Dylan's face she was pummeling but her own. Why did she have to be so prickly? Sure, Dylan had told her to go home, but he meant for her own safety. Didn't he?

Both of their parents had died young in a plane crash in South America, and she and Marissa had grown up with their grandparents. Their grandfather had always warned them that people would want to get close to them because of their money.

He'd even been convinced his son and his wife had been murdered.

So Mia had always made sure nobody got too close so she wouldn't have to question their motives. Then she spent most of her time buying friendships and loyalty just so she could keep things straight and stay in control. And it had worked with everyone…except Dylan and maybe his sister, Devon.

Dylan didn't want her stuff—didn't want to drive her Porsche, didn't want to cruise on the family yacht, didn't want invitations to the big parties with the live bands and fabulous guest gifts.

He had offered her friendship and protection over and over without ever asking for anything in return. No wonder she'd fallen head over heels in love with him.

Groaning, she pulled the pillow over her head. Peter had been right when he'd accused her of having a major crush on Dylan.

Peter.

What happened to him tonight? Did he fall? Did he jump? And why had Marissa's daughter shown up at this particular time? Unlike Dylan, Mia refused to believe that teenager had anything to do with the doll or the rock.

Mia's legs twisted in the sheets, and she stuffed the pillow beneath her head again. Strange forces were gathering in Coral Cove. Perhaps Kylie Grant, the fortune-teller, had stirred them up. Perhaps this sense of doom was the culmination of a summer soaked with murder and mayhem.

She shivered and tucked the ends of the blanket around her body. Maybe Dylan was right. She should finalize her decision about Columbella House and get out of town.

The sooner the better.

THE FOLLOWING MORNING, Mia flung open the drapes at her window and a blast of sunshine warmed her face, dissolving the previous night's fears.

She had a meeting with Linda Davis today at Columbella House to discuss renovation. She'd have dinner tonight to get to know her niece and make amends. She'd even send a sympathy card and flowers to Peter's sister.

Then she'd apologize to Dylan. She had no intention of pushing away the one bright spot in her life right now.

Showered and dressed, she leaned in close to the mirror above the sink in the bathroom to put on her mascara. Her cell phone buzzed on the tile counter and she checked the display. *Unknown.*

Hell, what wasn't *unknown* in her life right now?

She stabbed the button to answer and then the one for Speaker. Wielding her mascara wand again, she said, "Hello?"

A man's deep voice rumbled over the line. "Is this Mia St. Regis?"

"Yep."

"This is Matt Conner, friend of Dylan's. Do you remember me?"

"Yeah, yeah. Long black hair, motorcycle, surly expression."

He laughed, a booming sound that had her almost jabbing herself in the eye. "Nailed me. Dylan gave me your number when he asked if I could look into your sister's whereabouts."

"Yes?" A pulse throbbed at the base of Mia's throat. "Dylan said you didn't have time."

"No, I don't. Sorry."

Mia started breathing again as she brushed more black goop onto her lashes. "That's okay. Dylan's going to help me."

"I did have a chance to look into one thing, though."

Her heart rate ticked up again. "Oh?"

"Dylan told me Marissa took off for foreign parts when she left Coral Cove, right?"

"Yeah. I think she may have gone to Brazil, and then she was in Europe. The last postcard she sent me was from France."

"Uh-uh."

"Excuse me?"

"Didn't happen. She didn't go to Brazil or Europe, unless she went under an assumed name."

Mia moistened her dry lips. "How do you know?"

"I checked her passport records. Marissa St. Regis hasn't left the United States since she was twenty-one years old."

Mia dropped the mascara wand in the sink where it left a black smudge against the white porcelain.

If Marissa hadn't been sending her those postcards all these years, who had been?

And why?

Chapter Ten

"Mia? You there?"

She was here, but where was her sister? "Sh-she sent me postcards."

"Maybe she did, and maybe she traveled to all those places, but she didn't use her passport. Was she hiding from something...or someone? Is there any reason she'd be traveling on a forged passport with a different identity?"

"Of course not. Why would she do that?" A hard knot had formed in the pit of Mia's belly.

"Dylan told me she took off with some Brazilian con artist. Maybe that dude was in trouble with the law."

"Raoul?" Raoul had been on the lookout for a quick buck and a quick lay, but real trouble with the law? Doubtful.

"Do you have Raoul's last name? I can run a check on his passport, too. See where he's been."

Mia gripped the vanity with trembling hands. Did she want to know? "I don't want you to go to any trouble. Dylan said you were busy."

"Yeah, I have a full plate right now, but this seemed important to Dylan and I owe him big-time."

"You owe Dylan?"

"I had some trouble with my job, and Dylan stood by me. Even though he was going through that big mess in San Jose, he had time to talk me off a few ledges. Like I said, I owe the man."

Mia blinked at her reflection. "Dylan had a big mess in San Jose?"

"Uh, just on-the-job stuff. Do you have that last name?"

So she wasn't the only one who had a couple of secrets. "Neves. His name was Raoul Neves."

"I'll do what I can this morning and get back to you."

Before he ended the call, Mia sputtered. "Wait."

"Yeah?"

"You were here with Kylie Grant when she had that vision or feeling about my sister, weren't you?"

"I was there."

"How accurate are Kylie's feelings?"

He cleared his throat. "She can get confused. There was a lot of stuff going down last month, a lot of psychic turmoil for her."

"Stop dancing around. How accurate are Kylie's premonitions?"

He paused, and the line buzzed between them. Then he heaved out a heavy breath. "Pretty damned accurate."

She thanked him and ended the call. Clasping the phone to her chest, she stared at herself, wide-eyed, in the mirror. What did it mean? If Marissa hadn't been in Europe all those years, who was sending the postcards?

She swiped on some lipstick and then plucked her makeup bag and phone from the vanity and shoved them into her canvas bag. She'd have to tell Dylan about this new development—after she apologized.

Then maybe he'd confide in her about his real reasons for returning to a town and a job he'd sworn off years ago. Did it have to do with the trouble he'd experienced in San Jose?

Mia popped her head in the front office and called out to Gladys. When she didn't get an answer, she hit the bell on the counter.

Gladys peered around the door to the back. "Everything okay, Mia?"

"Everything's fine, Gladys. Just checking in on you."

"Seems you're the one who needs checking up on." Her nose twitched.

"I'm fine. What do you mean?"

"I heard about that ex-husband of yours. Why do people always make their way to Columbella House to kill themselves?"

"Good question, if that's what happened to Peter."

"Are you suggesting murder?" She pursed her lips. "We've had enough of those this summer."

"Maybe Peter's death was just an accident. He leaned too far over the railing, got vertigo and tumbled forward. It happens."

Gladys nodded. "Lots of things happen. Look at my Thomas. Got drunk one night and crashed his car on the Coast Highway."

"I know. I'm sorry."

Gladys's face sharpened. "Who was your visitor last night? Someone causing more trouble for you?"

The old gal wasn't as wrapped up in her gossip magazines and reality TV as she let on. Seemed she had a taste for some real-life gossip, too.

Mia sighed. The whole story was going to come out anyway. Kayla didn't seem too shy about claiming her roots.

"That was Marissa's daughter. She tracked me down."

Gladys's eyes lit up. "Doesn't surprise me a bit. Who's the father?"

Mia wasn't ready to out Charlie yet, not until he wanted outing. She shrugged. "Not really sure. Could've been someone Marissa met on that study-abroad program."

Gladys clicked her tongue. "But that would make the girl a foreigner, and she would've had a harder time tracking you down from overseas."

Nothing got by Gladys. "Who knows? Anyway,

I'm out for the day. I'm meeting Linda Davis at Columbella to discuss renovation."

Gladys snorted. "There's one woman who probably won't be too happy to hear about Marissa's love child. Could be her husband's."

"Tyler? I don't think so. He and Marissa were engaged after she gave birth."

"The mayor had a crazy crush on Marissa from way back."

"Crazy crush on her money,"

"That's your grandparents talking." She sniffed. "They had you girls believing that's all anyone ever wanted from you."

Gladys saw right through the St. Regis family dynamics. She must've seen and heard a lot working for the family over the years.

"Well, I have to run. Have a great day, Gladys."

"You, too, dear, and try to stay out of trouble."

Easier said than done. She smiled and waved.

On her way to Columbella, she stopped at a coffeehouse and grabbed a coffee and a yogurt parfait. While driving, she alternated between spooning yogurt into her mouth and checking email messages on her phone from her assistant. News of Peter's death had already hit the New York fashion scene.

She and Peter had been able to keep their acrimonious split out of the public domain, so at least nobody in New York would be blaming her for

Peter's death. The folks in Coral Cove, including that lieutenant, were a whole other matter.

She breathed a sigh of relief when she spotted Linda's Mercedes parked on the street. Not that she was afraid of entering the ancestral home on her own. She'd even had the electricity turned on and there were no protestors today, so maybe they'd be able to conduct their business in peace.

She parked behind Linda's car and approached the driver's side. Linda, head down, appeared to be checking her own messages.

Mia tapped on the window and Linda jumped. Guess she wasn't the only one on edge around here.

Linda buzzed down the window. "You scared me."

"Sorry. I thought you would've heard my car approaching."

Linda patted the hood of the car. "This baby's quiet as a tomb."

Mia clenched her teeth against the chill that rolled through her body.

"I'm sorry." Linda jerked her thumb behind her at the yellow police tape billowing in the ocean breeze. "Poor choice of words considering your husband's accident."

"Ex-husband." Mia's response was automatic.

"Well, not really. The divorce wasn't final. At least that's what I heard."

"Wow, you folks in Coral Cove are sure up on your gossip."

"More than you know, Mia." Linda flipped down the visor and dabbed at her lipsticked mouth. "Everyone now knows Charlie Vega fathered a child with your sister."

Mia's mouth dropped and she clung to the handle of the door for support. "How the heck did that come out?"

"The girl waltzed onto one of Charlie's construction sites and announced it."

Mia shoved her sunglasses to the top of her head and covered her eyes with one hand. "The recklessness of youth. How'd he take it?"

"You know Charlie. He took it in stride. Hustled the girl into his office and shut the door. When they both came out, there were smiles all around."

"I can't believe Kayla did that. The girl obviously has no self-restraint."

"Then the apple doesn't fall far from the tree." Linda reddened beneath her expertly applied makeup. "No offense, Mia, but your sister wasn't known for her discretion."

"No, she's not."

"Have you heard from her lately?"

"N-not lately. Having too much fun, I guess."

Linda snapped the visor up and dropped the tissue into the cup holder. "Let's go assess the damages in the house and talk renovation."

Both wearing high heels, they picked their way over the crumbling porch steps.

Linda pointed to the cement. "Starting here, this

porch could be replaced with a solid, gleaming wood. An awning above could protect it from the rain, but you'd need a heavy shellacking to protect it from the salty air."

Mia shoved the key into the lock, and Linda put a hand on her wrist. "These doors would look fabulous with a fanlight above."

And so it went. Linda made suggestions every step of the way throughout the house.

She'd obviously given a lot of thought to returning the house to its former glory. Her husband had probably encouraged her in the endeavor.

After they'd explored the upper floors, they paused by the basement door. Mia turned her back on the door and said, "Nothing to renovate down there."

Linda tried the handle. "Well, you can't very well restore the entire house and leave a dank, cluttered basement."

She hit the door with her hip and it gave way. She flipped on the light switch. "So much easier to explore since you turned on the electricity."

"Anyone home?" Dylan's voice poured into the silent house from the front door.

The sound melted the ice that had been creeping over Mia's flesh from the moment she and Linda had stopped by the basement door.

Linda murmured, "Chief Reese to the rescue again."

"Over by the basement, Dylan." Mia took a few

steps into the hall, her gaze settling on the welcome sight of Dylan striding into the house in full uniform, gun, handcuffs, billy club and pepper spray strapped around his hips. All the accoutrement a girl could get used to.

Linda turned, leaning against the basement doorjamb. "Are you taking up residence here, Chief?"

"No. I tried calling you, Mia, but you didn't pick up your cell phone. I knew you were meeting Linda over here."

Mia patted her pockets. "Must've left my phone in the car. What's the emergency? News about Peter?"

"Not yet. News on the other front." His gaze shifted to Linda, and he coughed. "You know. Regarding our visitor last night."

Mia twisted her mouth. "I already got the news from Linda. Kayla announced to the world that she's the love child of my sister and Charlie Vega."

Dylan's broad shoulders slumped. "And here I thought I was delivering breaking news."

"Apparently, there are no secrets in a small town." Mia rolled her eyes. "We were just going to descend into the dungeon. Do you and your weapons want to join us?"

"Sure, but I don't know what there is to renovate down there."

Linda tsked before descending the stairs. "We can replace these stairs for one thing." She wrinkled her nose. "Clean up, knock out some of the rotting wood along the walls."

Mia followed her and then scooted closer to Dylan when they hit the bottom. "I suppose I could have a gigantic yard sale with all this stuff. Maybe there's some hidden treasure here. You know, like on those shows where they tell you some cracked vase is worth a million bucks."

Dylan took a slow turn around the room. "Wouldn't surprise me."

Linda tapped the toe of her shoe on the cement floor. "We could overlay this floor with something nicer, too."

Mia wrinkled her nose. "When Marissa and I came back here, we did pour some new cement on the floor when we replaced the sea door that leads out to the beach."

"Well, whoever did it, didn't do a very good job." Linda crouched down and swept a hand across the sandy floor.

"Uh, Charlie Vega did it."

"Oops." Linda straightened up and brushed her hands together. "It's just cement. Like I mentioned, we can lay down something nicer."

Mia brushed past Dylan to get to the stairs. She'd had enough of the creepy basement.

"Of course—" Linda trailed off and Mia stopped, resting her foot on the first step "—Charlie might demand a piece of the action now."

"Why would he?"

"You're not the only direct St. Regis descendant now, and Charlie's the father of the other one."

Mia hit her forehead with the heel of her hand. "Just what I need, another complication."

Dylan picked up Linda's pad of paper and pen she'd put on top of a box and handed it to her. "Are you ladies done down here?"

Linda winked. "Don't tell me you have the heebie-jeebies, too, Chief."

"It's not where I want to spend my afternoon."

Linda took her notebook from him and tucked it into the briefcase slung over her shoulder. "I think that about does it."

Mia continued up the stairs. "You've given me a lot of great ideas, Linda. I'll definitely count on you if I decide to renovate the old place."

"If?" She tugged on the jacket of her coral suit. "You mean I didn't convince you?"

Mia raced up the remaining stairs and took a deep breath when she stumbled into the hallway. "Is that you or your husband talking?"

"Oh, I'm just interested in the challenge. Tyler wants to preserve the house as an historic landmark."

As Dylan tugged the door closed behind them, he said, "I wonder why he hasn't tried to do that already."

"He might have done something about it this summer, but as you know, Coral Cove had a busy summer." Linda hitched her briefcase on her shoulder as her heels clipped across the floor to the front door. "We even had to cancel our vacation."

"That's too bad. Where were you going?" Mia held open the door and gulped in a lungful of fresh air. If she ever did renovate Columbella House, she'd probably never set foot inside it again. It stifled her.

"We were going to the islands in Greece. Never been there before, and I was really looking forward to it."

"That's the price you pay for being married to a high-powered politician." Dylan slid a glance at Mia and she almost choked.

"Laugh if you want, Dylan, but he was dealing with some heavy-duty situations this summer."

Dylan raised one eyebrow. "Really? Because I thought the Roarke brothers and Matt Conner handled those heavy-duty situations."

Linda clamped her oversized sunglasses on her face and her lips turned up in a tight smile. "They did the heavy lifting, but there was a lot of clean-up after those men cleared out, leaving dead bodies in their wake."

Mia stepped between them and thrust her hand toward Linda. "Thanks so much for your expertise today. Like I said, if I decide to renovate, you'll be my go-to gal."

Linda took her hand in a light clasp. "Think about it, Mia. Do we really need another resort-style hotel on the coast, taking up more land?"

"I will think about it."

She and Dylan stood side by side on the curb watching Linda's Mercedes roll up the street to the house she was listing down the block.

"That niece of yours has guts, charging right onto Charlie's work site and claiming him as her daddy." He wedged a finger beneath her chin and tilted her head back. "Even if she didn't look just like you and Marissa, you couldn't deny that St. Regis chutzpah."

Her cheeks warmed beneath his scrutiny. "Yeah, about that chutzpah, I'm sorry I attacked you last night. You know, I think it's great you're back in Coral Cove, picking up the parental mantle."

He laughed in her face. "No, you don't. You're wondering what the hell I'm doing back here when I swore I'd be battling real criminals in the big, bad city."

She dropped her lashes. "You don't owe me any explanations."

"Don't I?"

His gaze dropped to her mouth, and a pulse throbbed somewhere...below.

"I told you to get your business done and get out of Dodge for your own safety—and against my own selfish interests."

Her heart did a double backflip. "And your own selfish interests are?"

"Right—" he brushed his warm lips against hers "—here."

The blip of a siren had them jumping apart, and Dylan glanced up, his brow furrowed. "What the…?"

"Chief!" A young officer waved out the window, a grin splitting his face from ear to ear. "Just heard on the radio. There's a fight on Main Street."

Dylan pulled his sunglasses from his front pocket. "Couple of kids?"

The officer's grin got wider. "Nope. Mr. and Mrs. Charlie Vega."

Chapter Eleven

Dylan swiveled around to face Mia. "You wanna lay a wager on what the fight's about?"

"I think we'd both be betting on the same thing." She shaded her eyes and asked the cop, "Is...is Charlie's daughter there?" May as well put it out there. If Linda Davis already knew, everyone else in town did, too.

"You mean that cute gal with the nose piercing? Yeah, she's there."

"Oh, boy. I'm following you over, Dylan."

He shook out his sunglasses and shoved them onto his face. "Do you think you should get involved?"

"I *am* involved. That cute gal with the nose piercing is my niece."

Dylan placed his hands on her shoulders. "Don't let that girl lead you around by a nose ring just because you feel guilty about Marissa. You know nothing about her, Mia."

"Except that she's Marissa's daughter, and she

needs help." She slid from beneath his grasp and walked as fast as her heels would allow to her car. "See you over there."

Dylan obviously didn't find the situation too pressing, since he didn't flick on his lights and sirens. Still, Mia had to take the turns a little faster than she wanted in order to keep up with him.

Of all the people Marissa had slept with, Charlie had to be the father of her baby—freewheeling, volatile, hard-living Charlie. Not to mention he'd acquired a jealous wife along the way.

Coral Cove's Main Street extended less than a mile, and Mia spotted the trouble as soon as she turned onto the street. A crowd of people and two cop cars, including Dylan's, marked the spot. She parked at the curb and exited her car, craning her neck to see above the crowd, which surrounded a parked truck with its windows bashed in. Charlie's truck.

She dodged and ducked her way through the crowd until she had a clear view of the trouble. Dylan already commanded the scene—large and in charge. That was what she liked about him.

Tracing her lips with the tip of her finger, she smiled. That was *one* of the things she liked about him.

He held up a hand to Tina Vega, who was still clutching a Louisville Slugger. "Put the bat down, Tina."

She hefted the bat in her hand and tossed it onto

the hood of the truck, where it inflicted one last dent before rolling to the ground.

The other cop ran forward and scooped up the bat while Dylan made a move toward Tina.

"Hold on, Chief." Spreading his arms out to his sides, Charlie took a couple of steps toward his wife. "Come on, honey. Let's go home and figure this out. After three boys, you always wanted a daughter."

Tina's eyes popped and her face got redder. She seemed to be pawing the asphalt.

Maybe not the best approach, Charlie. Mia clenched her teeth and shot a glance at Kayla, who stood behind her father, a slight smirk on her red lips. Just like her mother.

Mia itched to shake her niece. *Lose the smirk, Kayla.*

Dylan was right. What did she really know about the girl? Kayla had tracked her down, sent an unfriendly, accusing email, and then followed her to Coral Cove without an invitation. Now she'd blundered into her biological father's life without any concern for the man's wife and children.

What else was she capable of?

But she was Marissa's daughter. And underneath all that makeup and the tough-girl attitude lurked a confused little girl.

"I'll take her in until things cool down, Charlie." Dylan had slipped his handcuffs from his belt and turned toward Tina.

Tina's face crumpled and she sagged against Charlie's battered truck. "How could you, Charlie?"

Charlie moved in and wrapped his big arms around his wife. "Don't be so upset, Tina. I didn't even know you when I was with Marissa St. Regis."

"Marissa St. Regis." Tina practically spit the name into Charlie's shoulder. "Why her, of all people? Everyone knows the St. Regis family and that horrid house are nothing but trouble."

"Whoa, whoa." Mia sprang forward. "As one of the last members of the St. Regis family and owner of that horrid house, I take exception to that."

"One of the last members, but not *the* last." Charlie leveled a finger at his daughter, who had lost the smirk and was following the action with wide, curious eyes. Had Marissa ever looked that innocent when she wasn't faking it?

Dylan stepped between Mia and Charlie, giving Mia a tight smile. "Do you want to press charges, Charlie?"

"Absolutely not, Chief." He squeezed his wife, a big woman who almost matched him in height. "We'll figure this out on our own."

"Just do it in private and stop creating a public spectacle." He gestured to the tempered glass in pieces on the ground. "And clean up this mess, or I'll charge both of you with littering."

Charlie nodded. "On it, Chief. Kayla, do you want to come home with us?"

Mia shot Kayla a look from beneath her lashes. "I don't think that's a good idea right now, Charlie."

"I don't think so either." Dylan tucked away his cuffs. "You folks go home and cool down."

With the show coming to an end, the crowd shuffled away, murmuring and shaking their heads.

Wedging her hands on her hips, Mia turned to Kayla. "Did you think barging into Charlie's workplace and spilling the beans was the best of way of telling him he had a long-lost daughter?"

Kayla caught her lower lip between her teeth. "Probably not, but I don't have anything to hide. Why should he?"

"That doesn't mean you have to air your business in public. How do you think his three boys would feel if they found out through the grapevine they had an older sister?"

"His three boys, my half brothers, are visiting their grandparents in southern California."

Mia's eyebrows shot up, and then she schooled her face into nonchalance. This girl had mad research skills. How did she discover half of this stuff?

"Do you need help?" Kayla skirted around Mia and crouched down to hold the dustpan for Tina Vega.

Tina eyed her with a closed expression on her face, and then dipped her head once.

Dylan put his lips close to Mia's ear. "You gotta

admit, Kayla acts just like her mother and aunt—brazen and fearless."

Brushing her ear where Dylan's warm breath tickled her, Mia scowled. "I was never as bad as Marissa, and you know it. You never ran to *her* rescue."

He tilted his head, and she stared at her reflection in his dark sunglasses. "I never saw the soft spots in Marissa. You?" He tucked her hair behind one ear. "You had them all over."

"But the soft twin prevailed, huh?"

"I never had any doubt."

"Chief!" The other officer waved the bat in the air.

Dylan chuckled. "I need to wrap this up before he hurts someone. Do you still want to have dinner with your niece tonight, or do you want to avoid the fireworks?"

"Oh, I'm still game. Why? Are you afraid?"

"I should be." He strode toward the other cop just as Mia's cell phone buzzed.

She checked the display and saw Matt's name. She still hadn't told Dylan about Matt's first bit of news. "Hey, Matt."

"Hi, Mia. Hey, I'm sorry about earlier today. I gave you a shock, huh?"

"You could say that." Dylan glanced at her over his shoulder and winked. She waved back. "It's the postcards."

"I meant what I said earlier. She could be traveling under an assumed name."

"She'd have no reason to do that."

Matt cleared his throat. "I don't know about that. I checked out that Raoul character, and he is one shady dude."

Mia gripped the phone harder. And she was the one who had brought him into Marissa's life. "Has he been traveling? Does he have a companion?"

"He hasn't been traveling much, at least not on his own passport. Look, she could still be with him and they're bopping around using aliases. Those postcards could still be from your sister."

"So are you saying you don't believe Kylie's vision about my sister, that she's dead?"

"Kylie's not right all of the time. She was face-to-face with a killer almost every day and didn't recognize it. Didn't sense it."

Mia huffed out a breath. "Thanks for your help, Matt. Dylan's just across the street. Do you want to talk to him?"

"I gotta go, but tell him hey for me."

She'd tell him a lot more than *hey*. Tapping the phone against the heel of her hand, Mia studied the cracks in the sidewalk. So Marissa went on the run with some international criminal so that they had to travel under assumed identities? It might explain why Marissa had never come home, had always been vague.

Mia shook her head. It sounded crazy. But what

was the alternative? Marissa had never been to any of those places and someone was sending postcards and forging her writing?

"Have you figured it out yet?"

She jerked up her head. The debris on the street had been cleared away, and the Vegas, even Tina, seemed to be carrying on a civil conversation with Kayla.

"Figured what out?"

"You're deep in thought. Who was on the phone?"

"That was your friend Matt. He's good."

"I know he is. Did he have something for you?"

"Yeah, but it's *not* good." Her hand trembled as she slipped her phone into her purse. "It's weird."

The lines around Dylan's mouth deepened as he took her arm. "You're shaking. Let's duck into this coffee place."

He steered her toward a seat by the window. "Do you want one of those frothy coffee concoctions?"

Mia smiled as the words tumbled from Dylan's lips. His presence could make just about any situation better. She explained in great detail what she wanted, and then settled in a chair with her back to the window.

He delivered her drink and slumped in the chair across from her, cradling a cup of plain, black coffee.

"No frothy coffee concoction for you?"

"I had my limit for the day." He smoothed a

thumb across the back of her hand. "Now tell me what Matt had to say."

"He actually called me earlier this morning. I just never had a chance to tell you, what with all the other excitement."

"He gave you bad news?"

Mia twirled her straw. "Matt checked up on Marissa's passport, and she hasn't left the country in over ten years. She never went to those places on the postcards."

Dylan's gaze pierced her over the rim of his cup as he blew on the hot coffee. "Was that Matt's conclusion? That she never went to those places?"

"He made some suggestion that she could be traveling under an assumed name."

"But you're dismissing that."

"Why would she do that?"

"Lots of reasons. Maybe she's involved in something with that Brazilian guy."

She took her first sip of the frozen coffee drink and pressed her fingers to her temples. "That's what Matt thought. He did some digging on Raoul, too."

"Find any dirt?"

"Some. He didn't elaborate, but he must've found enough to make him believe Raoul and Marissa could be flying under the radar."

His warm fingers entwined with her cold ones. "So maybe that's the case—not the best circumstance, but not the worst."

"It's all my fault, Dylan." Mia covered her eyes

with one hand, not willing to lose the comfort of his touch on the other. "If she's on the run with Raoul, that's my fault, too. If I had never hatched that crazy scheme, had never brought Raoul to town…"

The pressure of his fingers on hers increased. "You and Marissa both pulled some outrageous stunts. That was part of your charm."

She peered at him through the spaces between her fingers. "Just because I gave you lots of practice for your rescue techniques."

Dropping her other hand to his, she dug her short nails into his skin. "I'm not like that anymore, Dylan. I'm not that madcap heiress."

"You always had substance under that layer of froth." He tapped her plastic cup. "Sort of like that drink."

"I guess you always saw through the froth, didn't you? Because you were always there for me." She hunched forward, her nose almost touching his. "And I want to be there for you, too. You can tell me anything. Don't you know that by now?"

"You have enough going on. I don't need to burden you with my stuff."

She smacked the table with her palm, and his cup jumped. "I want you to burden me. Our…relationship has been too one-sided. You giving, me taking."

Leaning back, he folded his arms over his chest.

"I'm not your sister, Mia. You don't owe me anything."

She blew out a breath. "Now you think I'm trying to use you to feel better about myself."

"You're giving me whiplash." He rubbed the back of his neck. "Feel free to use me…anytime."

Her nostrils flared as her gaze trailed a lazy path from his bunched-up bicep across the material of his shirt, which tightened across his broad chest.

"I just might take you up on your offer." She glanced at her watch. "I'm going to review everything I discussed with Linda, and then I'll meet you at…Burgers and Brews?"

"How about Vinnie's Pizza? I don't want to take a teenager anyplace that has *brews* in the name."

"Aye-aye, Chief." She saluted and pushed back her chair. "Since we're coming from different directions, I'll meet you there."

"I'll pick you up." He held up his hands. "Just use me."

She snorted, but her mouth watered and it had nothing to do with the thought of pepperoni pizza.

Later that day, as the sun dipped into the ocean, Mia pulled the door to her motel room closed. If Dylan insisted on driving clear across town and down the coast to pick her up, she could at least be waiting in front of the motel so he didn't have to park and come in.

As was her habit during her stay, she stopped by the front office to chat with Gladys, who already knew all about the fight between the Vegas in the middle of the street.

Gladys's faded blue eyes brightened. "She took a bat to his truck?"

"She did." Mia covered her smirk with her hand.

Gladys chuckled. "That woman's never happy. How long has she been complaining about a household of boys?"

"I'm sure she would've preferred a daughter of her own." Mia absently pulled a brochure for hang gliding from the rack by the front desk. "Do you really think Charlie will welcome Kayla into his home?"

"The man does have a big heart…and a sizable debt."

The brochure slipped out of Mia's hands. "What does that mean, Gladys?"

"Your niece is an heiress, isn't she? Marissa hightailed it out of here with a bundle of money, and I'm guessing a couple of trust funds."

Trust funds she hadn't touched since she disappeared.

"Of course, Kayla will be entitled to some money. If not Marissa's, then mine."

Gladys clicked her tongue. "Like I said, Charlie has bills and Charlie's daughter has money."

"Do you think Charlie's just pretending to welcome Kayla with open arms?"

"No, I think Charlie's honestly thrilled to have a

daughter, and he'd go all out for a poor one, too—but a rich one's even better."

Mia swooped to the floor to pick up the brochure, and stuffed it back in the rack. "I'm going to wait for Dylan out front. Take care."

"Like I said before, you take care, too."

Perching on a planter in front of the motel, Mia crossed one leg over the other, swinging it back and forth, her sandal dangling from her toes.

Great, another contender for the St. Regis money. The fun just never stopped.

A pair of headlights flooded the road, and Mia recognized the rumble of Dylan's truck. She could just as well have met him at Vinnie's. Maybe Dylan didn't want to give up his image of her as the damsel in distress. Maybe he didn't know what to do with a steady, sure-footed Mia St. Regis.

She was more than willing to show him.

He pulled up to the curb and she grabbed the handle before he could come around and open the door for her—because she knew he would. One independent step at a time.

She hopped onto the passenger seat. "Hey, you. I trust you had a calm and civilized afternoon in Coral Cove."

"No more bat-wielding wives, if that's what you mean."

"Where did Kayla go? Not home with the Vegas?"

"She did leave with them, but Charlie invited a

bunch of folks over, so she's not alone with them."
Dylan pulled away from the curb. "You didn't have
a chance to talk to her? Tell her the plans for dinner?"

"I texted her and she got the message. I'm assuming *kk* means she'll be there."

He glanced at her out of the corner of his eye.
"Feeling a little mature with a teenage niece?"

"Watch it." She poked him in the ribs.

The rest of the way into town, she chattered
about the plans Linda Davis revealed for the house.
"She really put a lot of thought into the renovation."

"She and her husband the mayor have probably
been thinking about it for years. Tyler's just letting his wife do the work now. He's backed off on
a lot of issues."

Crossing her middle finger over her index finger, she said, "I heard Tyler and the previous chief
were like this."

"I think I told you they had their daily meetings." Dylan swung into a parking spot and rolled
his eyes. "I put a stop to that right away."

They sidled into the crowded pizza place and
nabbed a table beneath one of the TVs. Mia scanned
the room. "I don't see her yet."

Dylan put in an order for a couple of pizzas and
brought a pitcher of soda back to the table. He tilted
his head toward the door. "Fashionably late, and I
use the term *fashionably* very lightly."

Mia swiveled her head around and caught her

breath. Kayla looked just like Marissa at that age—same flair for the dramatic, same long, confident stride. God, the girl could be a model. Of course, right now she was modeling a pair of shredded Daisy Dukes with black leggings beneath, high-heeled gladiator sandals and a denim jacket.

Kayla scooted out a chair and plunked down, breathless. "Sorry I'm late. My friends and I were figuring out what to do later."

"Are there boys among these friends?" Mia poured a glass of soda for Kayla from the pitcher.

"Uh, yeah, but we're all just friends—with no benefits."

Dylan raised his brows at Mia, and she shrugged. "Hope you like pepperoni and everything but the kitchen sink. We figured we'd better order before it got too crowded in here."

Kayla looked around. "I like this place."

"So tell me how your meeting went with Charlie—your father—and why did you decide to blab about your relationship in such a public place, in such a public way?"

The pizzas came and Dylan passed some plates around.

Kayla took a huge bite of her piece before answering.

"Well, it wasn't a complete surprise to Charlie."

"It wasn't?"

"I tracked him down before, just like you."

Mia had a mouthful of soda and it almost fizzed

out her nose. "Charlie knew about you before you came to Coral Cove?"

"Uh-huh." Kayla picked several mushrooms off her pizza before taking another bite.

The fact that Charlie already knew about Kayla left a sour knot of worry in the center of Mia's stomach. Why hadn't he said anything? Now she suspected his comment about working on Columbella House had a double meaning. Did he think his daughter owned a piece of that property now?

For the rest of the meal, Kayla peppered her with questions about Marissa. And Mia was only too happy to oblige her. Talking about Marissa, here in Coral Cove, made her feel closer to her twin.

Wherever she was.

The three of them did damage to a pizza and a half, and Mia told Kayla to take the rest to her friends. "Where are you and your friends going?"

"Here and there." Her black-lined eyes widened. "None of us is old enough to drink, so don't worry about that. And none of us do drugs either." She framed her face with her hands, her fingernails tipped with dark purple nail polish. "Despite my appearance."

Mia tossed a napkin into an empty pizza tin. "I like your appearance—edgy, quirky."

Kayla jerked her thumb at Dylan, engrossed in a baseball game on one of the TVs. "Even the chief of police has a tattoo."

"Yeah, just don't ask him about it." Mia ran her hand up Dylan's arm.

He tensed his arm just like he always did when she touched the tattoo.

Kayla waved and stuck out her tongue. When Mia turned toward the window she saw a group of teenagers pressing their faces to the glass, squishing their noses and lips into funny faces.

"You could've invited your friends to have dinner with us."

"Thanks, but I thought it would be better if we just talked so I could find out some stuff about my mom." She rapped her knuckles on the cardboard pizza box. "Besides, they can have the leftovers."

Dylan asked, "Do you mind that I showed up?"

"No, I mean you knew my mom, too, and aren't you like, Mia's boyfriend or something?" She slurped the rest of her cola through a straw, unaware of the bomb she'd just dropped on the table between them.

Mia creased the paper napkin in her lap. "Umm…"

Leaning back in his chair, Dylan stretched out his legs, a smile playing about his lips. He finally took pity on her. "Yeah, something like that."

"Okay, that's cool." Kayla slid her jacket off the back of her chair and hitched her huge bag over her shoulder. "You know, I wish you could find my mom and tell her about me. I really want to meet her now, even though she did give me up."

"We're working on it." Mia stood up when Kayla

did and pulled her in for a one-armed hug. She and Marissa had never been demonstrative, but this girl could use a hug and it felt right, felt good.

Kayla's body stiffened for a second, and then she relaxed and hugged Mia back. "Sorry I've been kind of annoying, but Charlie didn't mind. He's cool, and I think his wife is going to be okay with me. They had a bunch of people at their house today to meet me."

"Just be careful." It was too late to warn Marissa but not her daughter.

Dylan held up his hand. "Call if you need anything."

"All right. Thanks for dinner." With a flip of her long dark hair and a flick of her purple painted fingernails, Kayla bustled out the door to join her friends in a group hug with a few shrieks thrown in for good measure.

"The resemblance to your sister is uncanny, and I don't just mean her looks."

"That's what worries me."

He scooted his chair closer to hers and brushed a wisp of hair from her cheek. "You turned into a mother hen overnight."

"Are you saying I'm trying to use Kayla for redemption, too?"

"I'm saying—" he twirled a strand of her hair around his finger "—you've taken to that girl. I'm not making any judgments."

"That's a first for you." She dabbled her fingertips along the lines of his tattoo. "Or maybe not. What happened to you up there in San Jose?"

"Maybe I grew up." He cupped her face with his large hand. "Let's get out of here."

A little quiver of anticipation fluttered in her belly. He had sorta kinda admitted to being her boyfriend. Now maybe he'd make good on that statement.

He pulled her chair out for her and they left the restaurant hand in hand. They bumped shoulders as they walked on the sidewalk toward Dylan's truck, and Mia had to hold on tight to keep from floating in the air.

By the time he pulled into the small side lot of the Sea View Motel, Mia had run out of nervous chatter. She felt like they were back in high school, only Dylan had shown no romantic interest in her then and she'd never felt good enough for him. This was new territory.

She'd put him on a pedestal back then, and now she knew better. Nobody belonged on a pedestal. Nobody wanted to be on a pedestal.

Dylan had stopped talking about halfway through the drive, and now he grabbed the keys from her hand as they charged through the courtyard.

He unlocked the motel door and flung it open. When he turned his gaze on her, the temperature of the night climbed several degrees.

Stepping inside, Mia turned to offer him something to drink, but couldn't get the words past her own parched throat.

He already knew what he wanted.

He pulled her flush against his body and ran a hand behind her head, his fingers threading through her hair. He planted his mouth against hers, walking her backward until the back of her knees met the bed.

Her lips parted and a breathy sigh passed from her mouth to his. His tongue toyed with hers, gentle and playful at first and then thrusting, seeking, demanding. Clinging to his neck with both arms, she sagged against his body.

He deepened the kiss, inflaming her, melting her core. As her body turned to jelly, his seemed to harden. She knew the arm supporting her back would never let her fall.

Still wordless, their mouths, lips, tongues and now hands doing all the talking, they pressed against each other. Where her body left off and his began, Mia hadn't a clue.

Dylan tugged at her blouse, a sheer wisp of a thing floating over a lacy camisole. His words raspy and deep in his throat, he said, "I want to see you. I want to see all of you just like I always imagined."

She raised her arms, and he pulled the top over her head. He flicked down one strap of the camisole and trailed his lips down her shoulder, the stubble of his beard scratching the delicate skin on the inside of her upper arm. She closed her eyes, losing herself in the contrasting sensations of smooth and rough.

The pads of his fingers skimmed up her bare back as he rolled the camisole off her body. He cupped one of her breasts with his hand and brushed his thumb across her nipple, which puckered and ached.

"Oh."

He smiled into her hair. "Does that feel good?"

"Mmm, but I know something that will feel even better." She grabbed the hem of his T-shirt and yanked it up, getting as far as his shoulders.

He reached behind his head and pulled off the shirt, tossing it onto the chair. She pressed her hands against the hard planes of his chest, and the sprinkling of dark hair tickled her palms. Leaning her forehead against his body, she inhaled his scent. The fresh smell of the soap couldn't mask the essence of Dylan—outdoorsy, salty like a brisk ocean breeze and all male.

She bared her teeth against his warm flesh and took a taste. Then she shifted her mouth and flicked her tongue over his nipple. He sucked in a breath.

Shoving his hands down her pants, he cradled her bottom and fitted her more closely against his pelvis, where she felt his erection straining against the confinement of his jeans.

She grabbed the top button and groaned. "Why

are you wearing button-fly jeans at a moment like this?"

"I forgot my tear-away polyester pants at the strip club."

She laughed and smacked his backside, thrilled that even in the throes of foreplay their relationship hadn't changed. She didn't want it to change, except for adding the sex part.

"I could totally see you on stage shaking it in a cop's uniform."

"Don't…give…me…any…ideas." With each word, he teasingly undid one of the buttons of his jeans until the fly gaped open.

She peeled open his pants, tugging them down over his hips. Then she slipped one hand inside his boxers and stroked him, skimming her fingernails over his smooth, tight flesh.

As she toyed with him, he bent his head and circled her nipple with his tongue once before sucking it into his mouth. A warm gush of pleasure seeped all the way down to her toes.

He pulled away from her and ran a finger along the waistband of her pants. "How come you're still wearing these?"

"Uh, my hands have been too busy to take them off, and they even have a zipper."

Dylan made short work of the zipper, and the lightweight capris fell to the floor, pooling around her ankles. He centered his index finger on her stomach and pushed her onto the bed. She fell onto her back with her knees over the edge of the bed.

Dylan kicked off his jeans and boxers and crouched in front of her. He pulled off her silky panties and tossed them over his shoulder.

A shudder rolled through her body when he wedged his hands on the insides of her thighs. Not one smart quip made its way from her brain to her vocal cords. How could she banter? She couldn't even breathe properly. Her breaths came out in spurts and gasps, and Dylan hadn't even started working his magic yet.

When his mouth met her heated flesh, she almost jumped out of her skin.

"Steady." His big hands pinned her hips to the bed, and he began his assault again.

This time she thrashed her head from side to side as his tongue explored her. She wouldn't be able to last two minutes if he kept this up.

Four, three, two…she exploded. Crying out, she threw her hands over her head as the liquid fire seeped into her bones.

Dylan kissed his way up from her navel, across her belly, made two detours to her breasts and then nuzzled her neck. She dug her fingers into his thick, brown hair, the light from the lamp on the nightstand picking out the gold highlights.

His big body moved over hers, and she marveled once again at the way his rigid lines and planes contrasted with her soft curves, as if made for a natural fit.

She smoothed her hands over his buttocks and a rash of goose bumps raced across his skin. He nudged her thighs apart with his knee, bracing himself with his arms on either side of her.

He breathed into her ear. "Tell me how you like it."

"I don't care, Dylan. Take me however you want me. I've been yours for years anyway."

He locked his gaze on to hers and thrust forward. He pulled out slowly and thrust again, this time brushing his chest against her breasts.

She curled her fingers into the solid muscle of his backside, urging him on, begging for more, faster, deeper, harder.

Sweat dampened their bodies, and she licked the salty ridge of his collar bone. He seemed to grow inside her, filling her up until she felt as if he'd always been a part of her. And now that she had him, she'd never want to let him go.

The excitement built in her body. Tension gripped every muscle. A hot coil tightened in her belly. Dylan drove her closer and closer to the edge, his own muscles rigid and tight.

He whispered her name once, and the sweet sound opened the floodgates. The tension broke, sending waves of ecstasy coursing through her system. Seconds later, he reached his own climax, and they rode out their shared passion together, feeding off each other, their bodies in sync as their minds had always been.

When the last cries had died on their lips, when their bodies lay limp and their desire was spent, they still held on to each other. Dylan had shifted from her body, but his leg hooked around her in a possessive manner and her hand rested on the inside of his thigh, casually close to a part of his anatomy she'd only dreamed about days before.

Dylan yawned and kissed her temple. "Tell me that wasn't a dumb move."

"Dumb?" Her fingers danced up his thigh. "*This* is not dumb."

"I'd told myself earlier, I wasn't going to let my libido get in the way of a helluva friendship."

"Guess your libido has a mind of its own."

"No kidding."

Mia plumped the pillow beneath her head so she could look at his face. "Do you have regrets?"

"Not yet, but I'm ready to try again and see if any regrets pop up after the second time, or the third, or..."

He skimmed his hands up her stomach and molded both of her breasts, tweaking and teasing her nipples until she felt her blood stir again.

She shifted onto her side and snuggled her back against his chest, relishing the sensation of his warm, bare skin pressed against her and the way her body fit snugly with his. She wanted to memorize every groove, bump and hollow.

He wound his arm around her waist and she threaded her fingers through his fingers. The tattoo on his arm flexed, almost mocking her, reminding her that despite their intimacy Dylan had a secret.

Was it time to test him, or should she leave it alone? She had to strike while his body remained wrapped around hers. She took a deep breath. "Are you going to tell me more about that ink on your forearm now?"

He ran his tongue along the outer rim of her ear. "Why ruin the moment?"

"It's the perfect moment." She placed his hand over her breast. "We're intimate. Your defenses are down."

He pinched her nipple as he growled in her ear. "My defenses are never down."

"They must've been at one point." She scraped her nails along the curve of the five that ended in an arrow at his wrist.

Rolling onto his back, he crossed his arms behind his head, and a chill hit her damp skin. Was he going to refuse to open up to her? Maybe all this oneness she'd felt with him existed only in her head.

He cleared his throat and trailed a finger down her spine. "When I was undercover with the Fifteenth Street Lords, I screwed up. Big-time."

Mia's cell phone buzzed on the nightstand, and she wanted to throw it across the room.

Dylan's finger froze on her back. "Are you going to answer that?"

"Do I look like I'm making a move?"

He sat up and reached across her. "With all the stuff you have going on in your life right now, you'd better at least check the display."

He did that for her and tapped her shoulder with the phone. "It's Kayla."

"That girl pops up at the most inconvenient times." The chill creeping across her flesh grew more pronounced as Mia scooted up against the headboard, away from the covers and Dylan's warmth.

"Hey, Kayla, do you want more pizza or what?"

Someone sobbed over the line, and Mia shot up straighter, banging her head on the wood behind her. "Kayla?"

"What's wrong?" Dylan tucked the covers around her.

"I-is this Mia St. Regis, Kayla's aunt?"

"Yes. Who's this?" The languid, sated feeling that had infused her body after making love with Dylan evaporated.

"You need to come quick."

The blood pounded in Mia's ears as she waved away Dylan's insistent questions. "What is it? Where are you?"

"We're at the beach, and…and I think Kayla's dead."

Chapter Twelve

Mia's face paled, matching the white sheets as she dropped the phone and rocked back and forth. "Not her, too. God, not her, too."

Dread pounded against Dylan's temples and he snatched the phone from the bed. "Who is this? What's wrong?"

"It's Kayla. We were partying on the beach and she collapsed. I think she might be dead."

Dylan could hear voices and cries in the background, and a guy's voice shouting, "She's breathing! She's breathing!"

Dylan pulled the covers over Mia's trembling body. Her teeth were chattering so much, she couldn't form any words.

"Have you called 911 yet?"

The girl wailed. "No. We're scared."

Drugs? Dylan's lips tightened. "Where are you? I'm going to hang up and call 911."

She gave the location of the beach below Columbella, near the sea cave. Dylan cut across the rest of her babbling. "You tell the paramedics exactly what happened, exactly what she smoked or ingested. You got that?"

"Yes, but we didn't…"

Dylan ended the call and clawed through the discarded clothing to find his boxers while he called 911. He gave the dispatcher the kids' location, and then sat on the bed next to Mia, still wide-eyed, her skin blanched.

He gripped her shoulder and gave her a little shake. "One of the boys said she was breathing. The paramedics are on their way."

His words broke the spell of her panic and she jolted out of the bed and scrambled across the floor, picking up articles of her clothing and yanking them on.

"Let's go. I have to be there. I have to be there for Marissa's daughter."

"I know you do. The paramedics should be there before us. She'll be okay."

Mia clutched his arm, her nails biting into his flesh. "She has to be."

Dylan drove his truck up the coast as fast as safety, and his position as police chief, would allow. He roared up Coral Cove Drive and skidded to a stop in the turnout for the lookout area, joining an ambulance and a fire truck, steam from their engines mingling with the fog.

Dylan grabbed Mia's hand before she began clambering over the rocks.

"Be careful. We don't need two accidents to-night." Was Kayla's situation due to an accident? Self-inflicted? The hysterical girl on the phone hadn't been much help.

The EMTs had a spotlight on the sand where Kayla's friends huddled. They'd already lifted Kayla to a stretcher and hovered over her with masks and bottles and pumps.

Mia whimpered and began mumbling to herself.

Dylan grabbed her arm to guide her down the rest of the rocks. "They'll do everything they can to help her."

The rest of the teens lifted drawn faces, their eyes black pools, when he and Mia hit the sand and began jogging toward them.

Mia ran to the EMTs working on Kayla and assaulted them with questions.

Dylan started with one of the boys, who at least wasn't crying like all the girls. "What happened to Kayla?"

"We don't know." The boy held up his bony hands. "I swear, sir, we weren't doing drugs or anything out here."

Dylan inhaled the air around the kids and didn't smell anything unusual except an abundance of cheap cologne. He studied the boy's eyes, which looked clear with normally dilated pupils.

"Tell me what happened."

"A-after Kayla left the pizza place, we just

walked up and down Main Street. Then…" He cranked his head around to the others.

The girls were busy hanging on to each other and crying on each other's shoulders, but the other boy in the group made a slicing motion across his neck with one finger.

"Screw it, Quinn, this is Kayla. I have to tell him everything."

Dylan nodded. "What did you do next?"

"We went into that place, Burgers and Brews. It was crowded, packed. Looked like a lot of college kids in there." He wiped a hand across his mouth. "So we sat down and ordered some beers."

Dylan ground his teeth. Great. Was he going to have to cite his friend Bryan for selling to minors? "Did they serve you?"

"No. The waitress carded us and we told her we forgot our IDs. She wouldn't serve us without it, so we were joking around and ordered Shirley Temples from the bar."

"So you drank Shirley Temples?"

"We had a couple of rounds, just messing around, and then we ordered some nachos. Kayla didn't eat any 'cuz she just had the pizza. She didn't have any Shirley Temples either. Just water."

Dylan shot a glance at the EMTs working on Kayla. They wouldn't be working on her like that if she were already dead. He wanted to hold Mia, comfort her, but he needed to get the story from Kayla's friends first.

The EMTs began wheeling the stretcher toward the rocks, and Mia peeled away from them and stumbled toward Dylan. "I'm going with her in the ambulance. Thank God, she's still alive."

"Do they know what's wrong with her?"

Mia hugged herself. "Poison. They think it's poison."

The boys swore and the girls stopped crying long enough to look up with shocked faces.

The girl named Taylor said, "How could that be? Kayla didn't even eat or drink anything at that burger place except water."

Dylan crushed Mia against his chest. "I'll go to the hospital later. But right now I'm going to grill these kids to find out what happened tonight."

"Please, find out anything that can help her." She dragged her hands through her hair. "I just found her. I can't lose her already."

He kissed the top of Mia's head. "Go. I'll be with you as soon as I can."

He turned back to the kids, who were whispering among themselves. "What happened after you drank Shirley Temples at Burgers and Brews?"

A tall girl with blond hair choked. "The cookies."

Dylan narrowed his eyes. "What are you talking about?"

The girl continued. "Kayla had a bag of cookies, homemade cookies. She's the only one who ate them."

A pulse twitched in Dylan's jaw. "Where are these cookies?"

"She threw them away in a trash can on Main Street. She ate two of them, said they were pretty bad and dumped them."

The skinny boy clutched his hair. "Can cookies go bad?"

Dylan closed his eyes and took a deep breath. "Where did she get the cookies?"

The kids looked at each other, and Taylor said, "We thought she got them from her aunt because she had them in her bag when she came out of the pizza place."

"She didn't tell you where she got them?"

"No."

The boy who had warned the skinny one to keep quiet stepped forward. "The cookies were in a plastic bag. I think there were four of them. She ate two of them at the table when we were eating the nachos. When we got outside, I asked her for one and she tossed them in the trash and said they were gross."

"Were you all with her before she met me and her aunt for dinner?"

Taylor said, "I think she was at her real dad's place."

"Can you remember where she dumped the cookies? Was it in a trash can outside of Burgers and Brews?"

The boy shrugged. "Probably."

Dylan pointed a finger and drew a line across all of them. "Do not leave town."

The tall blonde put her hands on her hips. "We wouldn't leave without Kayla."

"Her aunt's going to want to call Kayla's parents, too. Anyone have that number?"

Four cell phones magically appeared and Taylor got the number first. Dylan punched it into his own phone and before he left the kids, he jerked a thumb at the smoldering fire. "Make sure you put that out before you go. And you'd better all be telling the truth."

He turned his back on their scared faces and climbed up the rocks to the road. The ambulance had to be at the hospital by now, but he had a trash can to investigate.

On his way back to town, Dylan got one terse text from Mia: stable, not conscious.

How the hell did Kayla wind up with poisoned cookies? Had the target on Mia's back transferred to Kayla's?

There. He finally admitted it. Weird things had been happening to Mia ever since she got to town, starting with her brakes.

Ted, the mechanic, hadn't come back yet with the results of Mia's accident, and he dreaded his report. Brakes did not generally go out on rental cars. The rental companies gave those cars the once-over before renting them out again. They'd have a load of lawsuits otherwise.

But the question remained. Why? Was that hulking old house on the cliff worth anyone's life?

He cruised along the dark, empty streets of Coral Cove. All of the restaurants were closed. Only the glow from the local watering hole illuminated a patch of sidewalk.

Dylan pulled up in front of Burgers and Brews, zeroing in on the trash can on the sidewalk.

The mayor took pride in the clean streets of Coral Cove, and the city council had ordered trash cans positioned on almost every corner of Main Street. They even had a decorative look, with pebbled cement encircling them.

He reached for his flashlight under the passenger seat and pulled it out. His long stride ate up the sidewalk.

He aimed his beam of light into the plastic trash can liner, and it played over crumpled napkins, plastic cups, used tissues and other assorted debris.

He lifted off the top of the bin and gathered the edges of the plastic bag, yanking them together. He heaved the bag over his shoulder and crossed the street, heading for the police station.

When he pushed through the door, the sergeant at the desk glanced up. "How's that girl?"

"Stable but still unconscious." Dylan nodded toward the other officer. "Did Greg fill you in?"

"Possible poisoning." He pointed to the bag Dylan was swinging from his back. "What's that?"

"Kayla dumped the cookies she'd been eating in this trash bag. Can you throw me some gloves?"

Greg wheeled his chair to another desk and grabbed a couple of plastic gloves from a box. He bunched them up and tossed them over the counter to Dylan.

"You want me to do that, Chief?"

"You already gave me the gloves, Greg. I'll handle it."

Dylan dragged the bag to the back of the station. He spread some newspapers on the floor and ripped the bag up one side. After snapping on the gloves he pawed through the trash. Greg shook out another plastic trash bag and scooped up Dylan's discarded items and put them in the second bag.

"Nothing. No food items at all. Shouldn't there at least be a few doggy bags?" He sucked in the side of his cheek, tasting blood. "Greg, is that homeless guy still hanging around Main Street?"

Greg cursed. "Yeah, he is."

"Where does he hang out?"

"Since we started harassing him, he moves around a lot. Spends a lot of time at the beach. Sleeps there most nights, if he can get away with it."

"We need to find him." He sat back on his haunches and peeled off the gloves. "Get patrol on the radio and have them keep a lookout for him."

"You mean this wasn't some sort of accident?

Why would someone want to poison that little girl, Chief?"

"I'm not sure, Greg, but I'd bet any amount of money it has something to do with Columbella House."

After touching base with his two officers on patrol, Dylan rushed to the hospital. He found Mia in the waiting room, perched on the edge of a vinyl love seat, a half-full plastic cup of water on the table in front of her.

She jumped up at his entrance and threw herself at his chest. "I'm so scared, Dylan."

He smoothed her hair back from her flushed face, damp with tears. She'd really taken to her niece in a short period of time.

"What did the doctors say?"

"They pumped her stomach and put in a saline IV. They stabilized her. Her breathing is more regular now and not so shallow, but she won't wake up." She ended on a wail.

"That sounds like good news. Those kids should've called 911 right away, but at least one of them had the sense to call you."

"It's definitely not drugs, so they were telling the truth there. Were they able to tell you any more about what Kayla had eaten and drunk?"

Dylan braced his hands on her shoulders. "Cookies."

"Cookies?" Mia blinked. "What kind of cookies?"

"Homemade cookies. Did you notice anything at Vinnie's? The kids said she had them when she met up with them, after her dinner with us."

"No, but Kayla had a big bag with her. She could've had a four-course meal in there."

"Just cookies."

"Do the kids know where she got them?"

"If they did, do you think I wouldn't be there now? They thought she got them from you."

"Me?" Mia stepped back and stabbed herself in the chest with her thumb. "Have you known me to ever bake anything from scratch? And where would I have whipped those up at the Sea View Motel?"

"She went home with the Vegas after that altercation in the street."

Mia laced her fingers in front of her and twisted them into knots. "Tina Vega bakes."

"You think Tina could've baked up a batch of poison cookies and sent them along with her husband's illegitimate daughter and nobody would be the wiser?"

"Nobody would be the wiser if Kayla had died." Mia clamped a hand to her mouth as if she'd just realized Kayla's death could still be a possibility.

"But Kayla was with friends. Surely Tina would realize Kayla would tell her friends and even share the cookies."

"Why didn't she?"

"Why didn't she share the cookies? Said they were awful and dumped them in the trash."

Mia gasped and grabbed his arm. "What trash?"

"Way ahead of you, kid. I've already pawed through the trash outside Burgers and Brews, which is apparently where Kayla dumped the remaining cookies."

"And?" Her grip tightened.

"And they're not there."

"Could the kids have been mistaken? Maybe they're in another trash bin. They're not locals. Maybe they got confused."

"Maybe. I'm having the rest of the trash bins searched." He pulled her close again. "When Kayla wakes up, she can tell us exactly where she got those cookies."

She whispered into his T-shirt. "Why, Dylan? Why would someone want to harm Kayla?"

"She's an heiress now, just like you."

She stiffened in his embrace. "You think someone tried to harm her because she's a St. Regis heiress? She's fairly new to the fold."

"But very public. Because of the way she went about things, the entire town knows she's Marissa's daughter, your niece…Charlie's daughter."

"Charlie? He wouldn't hurt a fly."

"Even for millions? Look at Peter. You thought you knew him, too."

"You're going to question them?"

"Of course. Don't they have the most to gain from Kayla's…?"

Mia shivered. "It could be any of those crazy

people who feel so passionately about the house. Kayla might represent another obstacle to their goals for the house."

The door to the waiting room swung open, and Dylan's own doctor, Dr. Fitzwilliam, came through, his stethoscope dangling around his neck.

"Mia." The doctor nodded. "Dylan."

"Is she still okay, Dr. Fitzwilliam?" Mia looked ready to burst into tears again.

The gray-haired doctor ambled toward Mia and patted her arm. "Her prognosis is looking good. All her vitals have stabilized."

Dylan's pulse ticked faster. "Has she regained consciousness?"

"Not yet, but there's no solid reason why she shouldn't."

Mia slumped and Dylan rushed to her side and put an arm around her shoulders. "It sounds good, Mia. She'll be okay."

The doctor winked. "That's the spirit, Chief. Think positively. Nothing more for you to do here, Mia. We'll call you if there's a change in her condition."

"Can I see her before I leave?"

"Sure. Talk to her, be calm, be positive."

Mia rushed from the waiting room, and Dylan turned to Dr. Fitzwilliam. "Do you know yet what kind of poison was in her system?"

"Not yet. We're going to run some toxicology

tests and examine what we pumped out of her stomach."

"Cookies."

"Excuse me?"

"We think she ate tainted cookies."

"Could be. Do you have any idea who did this?"

"Not yet, Doc, but I'm going to find him…or her."

Dr. Fitzwilliam slapped him on the back. "I have no doubt you will. Your old man would've, too."

Dylan forced his lips into a smile. 'I can't spare any of my officers to guard Kayla's room. Do you have someone on this floor 24/7?"

"Don't worry. Nobody is getting in that room."

"Call me if there are any problems with security." Nodding, the doctor left and Mia returned ten minutes later, her face brighter than when she'd left.

"Feel better?" He rubbed her arms from elbows to shoulders as if trying to warm her up.

A smile trembled on her lips. "She looks like Sleeping Beauty."

"Then just like that other princess, Kayla will wake up."

"Maybe we should send that skinny kid with the bad acne in here to deliver the awakening kiss."

Chuckling, Dylan cupped her face. "That's better. Keep it positive. Now I'm going to take you… home."

"I wouldn't call the Sea View home, but it'll do."

"I'm taking you to my home. You don't need to be alone tonight, and I'm not spending another minute on the lumpy mattress at the Sea View."

She brushed a hand across his stubble. "You didn't seem to mind that lumpy mattress about ten hours ago."

Glancing at his watch, he grinned. "That was just three hours ago."

He helped Mia into his truck and slid into the driver's seat. His phone rang at the same time he started the engine.

"What now?"

He hated the way Mia's hands formed claws in her lap. She didn't need any more stress tonight.

He glanced at the display before answering. "Whaddya got, Sarge?"

"You know that homeless guy, Hank, who's been haunting Main Street?"

Dylan eased out a breath. Nothing to do with Mia or Kayla. "Yeah?"

"He's dead, Chief."

Dylan's stomach flipped at Gary's tone. "What is it? What happened?"

"The officers on patrol found Hank dead on a park bench. Looked like he'd been eating some leftovers from the Dumpsters."

"Go on." A sour knot formed in Dylan's gut.

"He had a plastic bag near him…a plastic bag with cookie crumbs in it."

Chapter Thirteen

This couldn't be good, not the way Dylan's jaw tightened and his hand clenched the steering wheel.

"Did the officers take it in for evidence?"

He mumbled a few more words into the phone and ended the call, dropping the phone in his cup holder.

"Everything okay? Sounds like someone died."

"Someone did die—a homeless guy named Hank."

"Sorry to hear that. I think I may have seen him on Main Street."

Turning toward her, Dylan put his hand on her knee. "Mia, Hank died after eating Kayla's cookies."

Her heart slammed against her rib cage and she caught her breath. "What are you talking about?"

"Hank would pick through the trash cans up and down Main Street for food. Seems he found Kayla's discarded cookies and ate them. My guys found a plastic bag with cookie crumbs in it near Hank's body."

"I-if the cookies killed Hank, they're going to kill Kayla, too." She clenched her teeth to keep them from chattering.

"Not necessarily. Kayla is young and strong. Hank was an old drunk with a lousy immune system."

"It would've been better if Kayla had never discovered her St. Regis roots." Her nose tingled and she pressed the back of her hand against the tip.

"Look, this is bad news for Hank, but maybe we can get some prints from the bag, or the lab can analyze the cookie crumbs to help the doctors treat Kayla. She's going to be okay."

"When are you going to talk to the Vegas?"

Dylan started his truck and maneuvered out of the hospital parking lot. "Tomorrow."

By the time Dylan got to his place, which was really his parents' old house, Mia's eyelids were drifting shut. Two days ago, the thought of spending the night with Dylan at his place would've filled her with giddy anticipation. Now she could barely drag her feet up the front steps.

"You're exhausted." He peeled the sweatshirt from her shoulders and took her hand. "I'm putting you to bed."

She mustered a small smile. "Ten hours ago, that had a whole other meaning."

He rolled his eyes and chucked her beneath the

chin. "That was three hours ago, and it can have any meaning you like."

She yawned, and he swept her up in his arms. She tucked her head against his neck as he carried her into his bedroom.

He settled her on the bed. When he started pulling off her shoes, she struggled to sit up. It wasn't supposed to be this way. She'd wanted to prove to him that she could stand on her own.

He yanked back the covers. "Crawl in here. I've got your back."

"I want to be here for you this time. You're always the one giving."

"You've given me more than you know. Let me do this for you."

She peeled off her pants and shoved them off the bed with her legs. "What have I given you?"

"Your confidence."

"You've always had that, Dylan Reese."

"But now I need it. You don't know how much I need it."

The following morning, Mia sat up in Dylan's bed, rubbing her eyes. She'd fallen asleep in Dylan's arms, and he'd held her all night long. Even with her world falling apart around her, she'd never felt so safe. Dylan had that effect on her.

The clinking, clanking and smells from outside the bedroom meant Dylan was still playing caretaker. He seemed to need to fulfill that role right now, and she was too tired to challenge him for it.

She felt for her cell phone on the bedside table, and held it close to her face to view any missed calls or messages.

Dylan had left his home number with the hospital in case Kayla's doctor called, but unless Mia had slept more soundly than she thought, no call had come through.

She did have a few voice mail messages, and she listened to them with a pounding heart and pent-up breath. Again, nothing from the hospital, but a few frantic calls from Charlie this morning. He'd heard about Kayla.

If the guy was acting, he deserved an award. He sounded genuinely distraught. Peter's sister had left a message, too. She sounded much less distraught, and she seemed to want to make sure Mia didn't have plans to make any claims to Peter's business or his photographs.

Mia would have to assure her that she and Peter had signed a prenup, which cut Mia out of any rights to Peter's photographs. And *she* had every intention of abiding by the prenup, even though Peter had tried to render it null and void.

Dylan pushed open the bedroom door and poked his head into the room. "Do you feel like some breakfast?"

"Yeah, thanks." She held up her phone. "Nothing from the hospital."

"I called this morning. Kayla's holding her own. She hasn't regained consciousness yet, but all other signs are good."

"And Hank?"

"The coroner will wait for the autopsy, but it looks like poisoning."

Mia drew her knees to her chest and wrapped her arms around her legs. "If Kayla had eaten all those cookies, she'd be dead right now."

"But she didn't, and she's not."

"Are you going to interview Charlie and Tina this morning? He left about a million voice mails for me. Sounded very concerned."

Dylan crossed one index finger over the other and held them in front of him. "You are not going with me. This is official police business."

"Don't worry. I have my own business today, besides going to the hospital and checking up on Kayla."

"You're going to look into what it would take to turn Columbella into a hotel? I mean, since you've looked at renovation already."

"Nope. I've made my decision."

"Without vetting the hotel idea? Linda must've given you the hard sale on the renovation plans."

"I'm not renovating." Mia shoved off the covers and hugged Dylan's T-shirt around her body.

Dylan shook his head. "You're going with the hotel without even looking into it?"

"I'm not turning it into a hotel either."

Crossing his arms, Dylan raised one brow. "No renovation. No hotel. What do you plan to do with Columbella House?"

Mia opened her arms, taking a deep breath. "I'm tearing down the whole thing."

Dylan's brow rose even higher. "You're tearing down the entire house? What are you going to do with the property?"

"I'm sending it back to nature, Dylan." As she uttered the words aloud for the first time, she felt a measure of peace. "I'm going to leave the land there for people to enjoy. Maybe turn it into a park."

"You *have* changed."

"I'd been thinking along those lines for a few days now. What happened to Kayla last night sealed the deal." She shook her hair from her face. "That house has caused too much trouble over the years."

"Now you sound like Kylie Grant. It's a house, Mia. It's the people who have caused the trouble."

"Maybe, but the people have left their mark on the house. It's not a happy place. Can't you feel it? Even my grandparents couldn't live there in the end."

He took two steps into the room and pulled her into his arms. "You do whatever you want with the house, and maybe you'll feel like coming home once in a while to visit your park."

She smooshed her tingling nose against his chest. She didn't want to think about leaving Coral Cove right now. Didn't want to think about leaving Dylan and coming home for a visit once or twice a year.

"Now that I've come to a decision about the house, I want to concentrate on finding Marissa. She has a daughter to meet. Can you help me with that, Dylan?"

At least if she had him working on her sister's case, she'd have an excuse to call him every week…every day.

He combed his fingers through her bed-head hair. "I'll help you. I still have those postcards. I'll give Matt a call and then start there."

She blinked and looked up into his face. He'd always been there for her and always would be. "I knew I could count on you."

"Always." He tugged at the hem of his T-shirt that she'd worn to bed last night. "Eat some breakfast before you go to the hospital. I'll touch base with you this afternoon about the Vegas."

Her arms encircled his waist. "You're not getting off that easy."

He ran his hands beneath the T-shirt and caressed her back. "Do you mean you want to have your way with me again between the sheets?"

She choked and tried to pinch at some nonexistent love handles. "That is *not* what I mean."

"Oh." His hands stopped their circular movements on the bare skin of her back.

"Before Kayla's friend called me last night, you

were about to tell me about this." She zigzagged a fingertip along his tattoo.

"Relentless." He dropped to the bed, pulling her onto his lap.

"It's a part of you, Dylan. A piece of the puzzle. A key to how and why you changed."

He creased the edge of the pillowcase several times before he started talking. "You noticed the same tattoo on Rocco Vick, the man who accosted you at the Sea View."

"Yes."

"And I told you Rocco was a member of the Fifteenth Street Lords."

"Uh-huh." She held her breath, hoping for more, afraid to move in case it broke the spell."

"And I told you I was a member of the gang, too."

Her breath rushed from her lungs. "You told me you were undercover."

"Undercover and embedded. I *was* a member of the Lords."

A little tremble rolled through her body. He must have been in danger every minute of his life. "Th-that must've been nerve-wracking."

"Something like that."

"The experience of being in a gang changed you? You got your fill of big city police work then?" She bit her bottom lip. Did she really want to know what he'd endured as a member of that motorcycle gang? Had he done anything to prove himself?

"It was more than that, Mia."

The folds of the pillowcase grew more intricate, and the hand that had been supporting her back slipped to the bed.

He cleared his throat. "I was responsible for a woman's death."

She closed her hand around his agitated fingers. She wanted to dismiss his claim. He was the kind of man who would take responsibility even when the blame lay elsewhere. But an easy dismissal of his inner torment wouldn't go far.

She needed to allow him to work through his pain, find expiation, just like she planned to do with her sister.

"What happened?" She slid from his lap and huddled in close to him on the bed, still keeping possession of his hand.

"I'd gotten close to a woman, a girl, in the gang."

Swallowing, she tightened her grip on his hand. She'd have to be strong to get through this.

He jerked his head. "It wasn't like that. Melody really was just a girl, and she had a scumbag boyfriend in the Lords."

"Rocco Vick."

"Exactly." He shifted on the mattress and she sank against his arm. "Melody wanted out. The drinking and the drugging made her sick, the violence sicker. I got a read on Melody and I approached her."

"She helped you?"

"I didn't ask her to. I offered her a way out. She was grateful and volunteered to feed me information." He clutched the hair at the nape of his neck. "I should've refused."

"But she wasn't a little girl, Dylan, and she wanted to help."

"My superiors encouraged me to pump her for information, to send her into dangerous situations."

"You couldn't refuse."

"They threatened to pull me out, and all those years I'd sacrificed to the job, the years I had to pull away from Devon and her son, they all would've been wasted."

She sealed her lips. Dylan didn't need to hear platitudes right now.

"So I followed orders. My intel was leading to some good busts, and the Lords started looking over their shoulders." Closing his eyes, he tipped his head back. "Then it all came crashing down."

"Someone blew your cover?"

"Melody blew my cover."

"She turned on you?"

His head snapped back to attention. "She had to. They caught her and…and forced the information out of her. I never blamed Melody."

"What happened to her?" Mia reached for a glass of water on the nightstand and knocked it over.

Neither of them made a move to rescue it and watched the water dribble down the nightstand and soak the carpet.

"The Lords murdered her."

"That man, Rocco?"

"No. I don't think he would've had anything to do with it, but he blamed me for Melody's death."

"He should be blaming his buddies in the gang." She leaned her cheek against his arm and hung her arm around his broad shoulders, stiff and tense. "Once your cover was blown, did they come after you?"

"They tried, but by that time, I knew about Melody. Then it was all over." Hunching his shoulders, he braced his hands on his knees. "My department pulled me out. Sent me to the department psychiatrist."

"Did it help?"

He snorted. "No."

"Did you even give it a try, Dylan? It might have helped." She couldn't see Dylan Reese pouring out his fears and insecurities to a shrink, but other cops did it.

"The only thing that helped was coming back to Coral Cove. These people have faith and confidence in me."

She nuzzled his ear and whispered, "I have faith and confidence in you, too."

"Still?"

"Is that why you were hesitant to tell me about the tattoo and Melody? Did you really believe your experience would make me think any less of you?"

"It should. I caved to the brass and got a woman killed."

"You were doing your job, and as sweet and helpful as Melody may have seemed to you, she'd hooked up with a man like Rocco Vick and willingly stepped onto the dark side." She shook his arm. "Not every woman is a blameless damsel in distress waiting for your charge to the rescue."

"Like you?"

She flopped back on to the bed. "Especially not me. In fact—" she covered her face with her hands, muffling her words "—I kind of played you all those years ago."

He lay back next to her and kissed her cheek. "I know that, Mia St. Regis. And I liked it."

She turned her face to his and their lips were so close, all she had to do was pucker. He kissed her long and hard, and his tense muscles relaxed.

She'd done that for him. And she'd continue doing that for him any way she could. For as long as she stayed in Coral Cove.

He rolled from the bed and grasped her ankles, which were hanging over the edge. "You haven't even had breakfast yet, and I have to get going."

"I can lock up after I eat." She sat up. "You need to talk to the Vegas."

"I don't want to leave you here on your own." He tugged on her legs. "You don't have your car anyway."

She fluttered her feet, her ankles still in his light

grip. "You don't want to leave me here on my own? Are you afraid I'll go nosing around and discover all your deep, dark secrets?"

"You already know all my deep, dark secrets." He dropped her ankles. "Are you forgetting that someone tried to poison your niece last night?"

"How could I forget that?"

"Peter. Kayla. Seems to me, people close to you have big bull's-eyes on their backs, and you haven't escaped either."

"Getting a voodoo doll doesn't compare to getting poisoned, and I really think that doll was Peter's touch."

His blue eyes darkened and his jaw tightened. "Both Peter and Kayla are connected to you, Mia, and you're all connected to that house."

"Back to Columbella House again? Do you seriously believe someone cares enough about what happens to that house to kill for it?"

"Did you get a load of those protesters? And the rock?"

She touched her chin. "It's crazy, Dylan. I know some people want to see that house restored and some want me to tear it down and put up a hotel, but if one or the other of those things happens, it's not exactly going to be the end of the world for someone."

"Money."

"Are you throwing that out there as a motive?"

"Sure. Money and love—the two biggest motivations out there." He scratched his stubble. "Think about it. Who stands to gain some money out of either of those deals?"

"Well, anyone I would hire for restoration or construction, but I could employ those people either way, and the town stands to benefit either way, too. It seems to me it's more a struggle between the traditionalists, who want to preserve some history, and the modernists, who want to draw a different kind of tourist to the area. Hardly the stuff to inspire murder."

"And yet that's what we have."

"Once I make it clear I'm not taking either route, I'd better hire a bodyguard."

"You've got one of those." He pulled her up from the bed and kissed her. "When are you breaking that bit of news?"

"I'm going to drop by the city planning office today and find out what it will take to turn Columbella into parkland and donate it to the city. I'm sure word will get out soon enough."

"I think you're right. Get dressed and eat some of those cold eggs. I'll drop you off at the Sea View." He swept the stack of Marissa's postcards from his dresser and shook them at her. "I'll start working on this, too."

"You're a man of many talents, Chief Reese."

He quirked his eyebrows up and down. "You have no idea."

"You won't toss me out of your truck if I skip a shower, will you?"

"Not at all, but I draw the line at no teeth brushing. I have a few new toothbrushes in the middle left drawer in the bathroom."

"Okay, let me shovel down some of those eggs first." She sniffed the air. "Is that coffee I smell?"

"Yep. Get it while it's hot, or lukewarm."

Mia followed him out of the bedroom and hopped up on a stool at his kitchen counter, tugging at the T-shirt as it rode up her thighs.

He held up a plate of scrambled eggs. "Do you want me to zap these in the microwave?"

"No, I'm good."

He put the plate in front of her and shoved a coffee cup next to the plate. "Milk and sugar?"

"Just milk."

The phone rang and Dylan's hand jerked, spilling milk over the side of the cup. "Sorry."

He grabbed a dish towel and tossed it to her, and then answered the phone.

"Hey, Ted. What's up?" He put his hand over the phone and mouthed, *The mechanic.*

Mia nodded and wiped up the spill. She dumped a little more milk into the mocha-colored liquid and took a sip.

"You did?" Dylan dropped the glass he'd been rinsing in the sink, and Mia's gaze shot up. "I'm putting you on speaker phone, Ted. I want Mia to hear this."

Ted's raspy voice scratched over the line. "Hi, Mia. I've been looking at your rental car. The rental car company wanted me to take a look, and I think I figured out why you crashed into that guardrail."

Mia's pulse quickened. "I know why, Ted. The brakes failed, so if the rental car company's trying to prove it was my fault, I'll dispute it all the way."

"No, it's nothing like that, Mia." Ted expelled a long breath. "What I was just about to tell the chief is, I know *why* the brakes failed."

"Why, Ted?"

"Someone cut the brake lines."

Chapter Fourteen

Mia felt the blood drain from her face, and her hand shook as she put down her coffee cup with a clink.

Dylan said, "Are you sure, Ted? The car was a mess when it came up."

"Yeah, I know that, Chief. But only one portion of the car burned. Things were pretty mangled, but I did get a look at the brake lines, and it looks like a clean cut to me."

"I'm going to come by and have a look."

"That's fine. This car ain't going anywhere. And, Mia?"

She licked her lips. "Yeah, I'm still here."

"You better watch your back."

When Dylan ended the call, Mia slumped over the counter. "Oh, my God. So you really think somebody tampered with the brakes on my rental car?"

Dylan looked ready to snap the phone in two. "Ted's a good mechanic."

"But he's working for the rental car agency. They put him up to it."

"Do you think he just came up with that story to get the car company off the hook? Ted doesn't operate like that."

"Maybe they paid him off."

Dylan walked around the counter and squeezed her shoulders from behind. "I know you don't want to believe it, Mia, but it makes sense."

She twisted around on the stool. "It doesn't make any sense at all. Why would someone want to kill me or my niece or my ex-husband for a house?"

"I don't know. What happens to the house in the event of your death?"

"I'm not sure. I'm the only heir. It wouldn't go to anyone in any of the other branches of the St. Regis family."

"But if Marissa could be found, it would go to her?"

"Yes."

"Where is Marissa, Mia?"

"That's what I'm trying to—" Her jaw dropped. "You're not implying that Marissa is back and skulking around to get the house from me."

"N-no."

Hooking her legs around the stool, she crossed her arms. "You'd better not be. That's ridiculous. Then she, what? Decided to kill her own daughter while she was at it?"

"Sounds crazy."

"Glad you think so."

"Let's think about this. Someone comes after

you first. Your husband shows up in town, offering another obstacle to the house. He publicly threatens to take it from you, and he dies."

"He could've committed suicide. He really did have financial problems."

"We have no results from the autopsy yet." He took a turn around the room and landed in front of her again. "Marissa's daughter makes an appearance next. Again, very public, everyone knows who she is—another possible St. Regis heiress. She eats poisoned cookies."

"Now I'm the only one left."

He leaned against the counter, an arm on either side of her body, imprisoning her. "You need to call your attorney and find out who gets the house when there are no more direct St. Regis heirs."

"I just can't believe anyone would go to those lengths."

"Look at you. You tricked your sister out of a marriage and entered your own loveless marriage of convenience—all for that house."

"Don't remind me."

Pressing his forehead against hers, he said, "Your announcement of your plans for the house is either going to make one interested person very happy...or very angry."

MIA'S SANDALS SLAPPED the hospital corridor as she inhaled the sweet fragrance of the flowers she clutched in one hand. Kayla's doctor had al-

ready told her that Kayla's condition remained un-
changed—stable but still in a coma.

She pushed open the door to Kayla's room and
peered inside, her breath catching in her throat
when she caught sight of the tubes running into
Kayla's arm. She'd be safe in her parents' home in
Arizona if she hadn't come on this road trip to meet
her biological family. And if her mother hadn't disappeared off the face of the earth, maybe she'd be
enjoying a reunion with her right now.

It all came back to that moment when Mia had
decided to trick her twin.

She pasted on a smile, even though Kayla
couldn't see her, and tiptoed into the room, even
though Kayla couldn't hear her. "Good morning,
Kayla. I brought you flowers. Your friends are really worried about you. I talked to them this morning."

She kept up the cheerful chatter. Even if Kayla
couldn't distinguish her words, Mia wanted to project a positive tone. She wanted to send out rays of
hope.

Ted the mechanic had dashed any hopes Mia had
been harboring that the events of the past few days
added up to some crazy coincidence.

*Someone had cut the brake lines to her rental
car.*

She shivered and glanced over her shoulder at
the silent hospital corridor. Who could possibly

want Columbella House so badly and for what purpose?

If she knew, she'd gladly hand it over. The house meant nothing to her now—worse than nothing. It had become an albatross of her own making.

She continued sitting with Kayla until the nurse, Geri, came into the room. "I know she's not responding now, but having you here does help."

"Do you think she'll come out of this okay?" A tear trembled on the edge of Mia's lashes. Through the blur of tears, Kayla looked even more like Marissa.

Geri patted Mia's back. "I've seen plenty of miracles. Physically, she's out of the woods, so that's a good sign. Sometimes people just wake up, no rhyme or reason. Just miracles."

Mia sniffled. "Thank you. I'll keep praying for that miracle."

She walked to her car in the parking lot while checking her cell phone. If Dylan had gotten anything out of the Vegas, he'd have called her by now. Charlie Vega might be interested in the St. Regis riches, but he'd seemed genuinely thrilled with his surprise daughter and genuinely upset at her poisoning.

Mia drove back to downtown Coral Cove and pulled into one of the slots in front of City Hall. She'd called ahead to set up a meeting with the city planning commissioner, Dirk Fielder. He met her at the window of the planning office.

"Come around to the side door, Ms. St. Regis."

"Call me Mia." She tucked a notepad under her arm and waited by the door.

He ushered her into a small office in the back and snapped the door closed. "Lots of nosy people around this office. I'm assuming you're here because you've made some sort of decision about Columbella House."

"That's right." She smacked her notepad on his desk blotter.

Leaning back in his chair, Fielder steepled his fingers. "So what's it going to be? Restoration of a city icon or another beachfront hotel?"

"Neither. I'm going to tear down the house and turn the land over to the city for a public park."

Fielder's brows shot up to his sandy hairline. "You're kidding."

"Nope. I'm sick of the house. I don't want to deal with it anymore. There's a beautiful view from that spot, why shouldn't everyone be able to enjoy it?"

"I'm all for that." He swung his computer monitor around to face him. "Let's see. We're going to have to check out the zoning, traffic, parking, all sorts of boring details."

"I'll let you handle the boring details, Mr. Fielder."

"Call me Dirk, since it looks like we'll be spending some time together."

They started with an hour and a half. Dirk knew

his stuff, and by the time Mia left the uncomfortable chair in his office, she knew she'd made the right decision.

Now she just had to convince everyone else of that fact.

She turned the corner from the planning office and ran smack into Jimmy Holt, boy journalist.

Mia's notebook and papers, along with Holt's, scattered all over the yellowed linoleum floor. They both reached for their stuff, nearly banging heads.

Mia pulled back. "Do you cause trouble wherever you go?"

Flashing a smile, he said, "I try to."

She scooped up a few papers and sorted through them, pulling out Jimmy's notes. She thrust them toward him, still crouching on the floor. "These are yours."

His nose was buried in a sheaf of papers. "And these are yours. Columbella House a park?"

So much for keeping her plans secret. She blew at a strand of hair stuck to her lipstick. "Maybe."

He waved the papers in the air. "This is big news. I wonder how the two opposing sides are going to feel about this."

"Don't know." She snatched the papers from his hand. "And don't care. It's my house."

"Yeah." He pushed to his feet, scratching his chin. "It *is* your house."

She shoved his papers into his midsection. "That's what I just said."

He gathered his forms from her and smoothed out the corners with care. "It's your house even after that threat from your husband and the appearance of your niece on the scene. Still your house."

"I know you're longing to sharpen those journalistic skills by reporting on something more than the annual 5K run for education, but there's no story here."

"I've had plenty to report on this summer—a serial killer, a couple of murderers down from the city and a cold-case murder."

"Yeah, is the *New York Times* calling you yet?"

He folded his arms, hugging the papers to his chest. "I'm happy right here, and now I've got my lead story for tomorrow."

"Ooh, and bump your stellar piece on the firemen's picnic?" She rolled her eyes.

"The firemen can wait. Everyone wants to know what's going on with Columbella House." He spun around and whistled down the hallway.

Mia shrugged and meandered off in the opposite direction. The good people of Coral Cove were going to find out what she intended for Columbella House anyway. It was just going to be sooner rather than later, and while she was still in town.

And still within reach of whoever cared enough about the fate of the house to kill over it.

DYLAN PUSHED UP his sunglasses onto the bridge of his nose and jotted a few more notes in his book. Charlie had seemed upset, and even Tina had shed a few tears over Kayla's condition.

Neither one of them knew anything about any cookies, and claimed that Kayla didn't have any with her when she'd been at their place yesterday. Tina claimed the only cookies she'd served at their little gathering were store-bought.

So where had Kayla gone after leaving the Vegas' and meeting Mia and him for dinner?

He wanted Mia out of town. If someone had designs on Columbella House, that someone wouldn't be too happy to discover Mia's plans for a park. Or maybe that would be just the ticket.

What did this person want? There had to be more to the story than just a desire to see a house preserved or another ocean-view hotel on the coast.

Before he started the engine, he pulled his cell phone from his pocket. A missed call from Mia. She was probably hoping he'd found a batch of poison cookies at the Vegas' place. He'd have to disappoint her.

He didn't like disappointing Mia. She'd handled his confession about his role in Melody's death well. Hadn't tried to talk him out of his guilt. Nobody could do that.

But she hadn't lost faith in him. Her dark eyes

still shone with trust and confidence when he assured her he'd continue to look into the mystery of Marissa's disappearance.

He reached into the console of his squad car where he'd stashed Marissa's postcards. He thumbed through them, comparing the writing on the backs of the cards. Identical. The same person wrote all of the cards. Was it Marissa?

He flipped the cards over, and the setting sun glinted off the shiny surfaces, blending the colors of the azure seas and emerald foliage. Anyone could've bought these postcards from any location.

He traced the postage in the upper-right corner of the cards. But no one could fake the metered stamp across the postage. These cards had been sent from these locations—no doubt about that.

Matt could be right. Marissa could be on the run, living under an assumed name. Why else would she stay away for so long? She and Mia had never been close, but Marissa wouldn't have stayed away so long.

Dylan didn't buy Mia's fears that Marissa had stayed away all these years out of anger over the stunt Mia pulled. Marissa would've been the first one to get a kick out of it.

Marissa had no interest in Columbella or the family history. Besting your twin had been a game the two St. Regis girls had played for as long as Dylan could remember.

The game had landed Mia in more than a few

scrapes, scrapes that he'd been only too happy to rectify for her. His lips twitched into a smile. He was still rescuing her, and contrary to her belief, he didn't mind at all.

His cell phone rang on cue. "I'm outside the Vegas' house, and no, nobody confessed or offered me milk and cookies. How's Kayla?"

"Stable, no change."

"That's not the best news, but it's encouraging. She'll come around."

Mia sniffled, and Dylan knew she'd replaced Marissa with Marissa's daughter. If she lost her niece, too, Mia would never be able to forgive herself. Dylan would never be able to bring her back from that.

"The nurse seemed to think Kayla could regain consciousness at any time."

"There you go. Keep your chin up."

"So you didn't get anything from Charlie and Tina?"

"Charlie's worried sick, and even Tina is upset. I don't think they had anything to do with poisoning Kayla."

"I don't even care where she got the cookies now. I just want her to wake up." Her words ended on a sob, and Dylan ached to be with her to soothe way the pain.

The woman had reeled him in again, and this time he didn't think he could let her drop the line and walk away.

"I care where she got the cookies. The person who gave her those cookies is still out there, and I'm sure would like to do some baking for you, too. Also, don't forget. The cookies killed Hank. We have a murderer on our hands."

"And Peter? Any word on his cause of death yet?"

"We won't have anything back for a few weeks, but you're right. We may have a killer times two."

"It's crazy, Dylan."

"The person who's doing this is crazy." He tossed the postcards onto the passenger seat of his car. "But you can let the Coral Cove P.D. handle this. Make your arrangements for the property, and go home. I'll be in touch—a lot. If Kayla doesn't regain consciousness before you leave, you can make arrangements to have her moved to a hospital in Phoenix. Did you call her parents yet?"

"Y-yes."

"What's wrong? They didn't blame you, did they?" His hand fisted around the steering wheel.

"Not at all. They knew Kayla had embarked on this quest, and they were okay with that. They're assuming Kayla's poisoning was an accident. I didn't go into too much detail with them."

"They must be worried sick."

"They are. They're coming out as soon as they can get a flight."

"So, what's the problem? You sounded…funny."

She coughed. "My scheme to put my plans fo

Columbella in motion and then hightail it out of here sort of fell apart."

He clenched the steering wheel again. "How so? The city zoning won't allow for a park located on Coral Cove Drive?"

"That's not it. Mr. Fielder in the planning office was thrilled with the idea."

"Get to the point, Mia. What's the problem?"

"I ran into Jimmy Holt at City Hall—literally, ran into him. My papers flew out of my hands, his papers flew out of his hands…"

"He found out about your plans."

"Yep."

Dylan swore and hit the steering wheel with the heel of his hand. "Is he going public with them?"

"He wouldn't be Jimmy Holt, boy journalist, if he wasn't—front-page story in the *Coral Cove Herald* tomorrow, no less."

"Maybe I can pay him a visit and convince him otherwise."

"You'd use your power and influence for me?" He could almost hear her fluttering her eyelashes. "Maybe you could flex that tattoo a few times."

"You're not taking this seriously."

"Look, you're not going to convince Jimmy the journalist to hold that story, and we don't even know how my plans are going to affect the person who poisoned Kayla. Maybe he'll be happy. Maybe he's some kind of environmentalist nut who's been pulling for the whole thing to come down anyway."

Dylan heaved out a breath and closed his eyes. "I don't like it."

"Neither do I, but it is what it is. I'll be done this week, anyway. I have a few more meetings to take, and I need to make arrangements for Kayla. Then I'm going back to New York, and I think it would be pretty obvious of someone from Coral Cove to follow me there."

"Not if you don't know this person."

"Are you telling me it could be some stranger?"

"You don't know every resident of Coral Cove, Mia, especially now. This person could be someone totally unknown to you."

"Thanks. You just made me feel a whole lot better."

He eased the car away from the curb and put his cell on Speaker. "Why are we sitting here talking on the phone when all I want to do is take you in my arms?"

"Really?" Her voice squeaked. "Because that's what I was thinking, too."

"Meet me for dinner in town."

"The Whole Earth Café in fifteen minutes?"

"If you insist, but give me forty-five. I need to drop by the station."

"You got forty-five, Chief."

Dylan returned to the station to check in and enter his notes from the Vega interview into his computer. One of his officers told him they'd have to wait a few weeks for Hank's autopsy, too. Things moved at a snail's pace in small towns since they had to depend on bigger departments for most of their lab work.

He hoped to God Mia was safely back in New York before he got either Peter's or Hank's autopsies back. Then he snorted. That's probably the first time anyone would suggest someone leave the dangers of Coral Cove for the safety of New York.

He stepped inside the Whole Earth Café, its interior filled with plants and cooled with a ceiling fan. The weather usually started heating up on the coast in September. He'd missed the beginning of the summer when fog typically socked the town.

Mia waved to him from across the room, as if he hadn't already spotted her. As if she didn't completely light up that little corner. As if she didn't send out an electric current that zapped him to his toes every time he saw her.

And if she didn't stay?

He adjusted his heavy equipment belt and strode across the room. That wasn't an option.

Her eyes widened at his approach. "You look like you're ready to arrest me."

That would work to keep her in town—once he got rid of the threat to her and her family.

"That's my hungry look. I'm starving."

She spread her hands. "You can get just about anything here. Don't let the decor fool you."

"I know that." He pulled out a chair across from her and collapsed in it. "Don't think I haven't been to every Main Street restaurant at least once since I moved back here."

"I started without you." She held up a glass of iced tea.

The waiter stopped by and Dylan ordered some tea and some sweet potato fries.

"How did Kayla look?"

"Like she was sleeping…and just like Marissa."

"That's why you've bonded so quickly with her."

"You have to admit—she's kinda likable."

"Kind of a pain in the rear end."

"Just like Marissa."

Cupping her face, Dylan traced her jaw with his thumb. Her big eyes always drooped when she mentioned her sister. He had to figure out where the hell that woman had gone off to.

"Tell me what Dirk Fielder said about Columbella Park."

The straw popped out of her mouth. "Did I say I was calling it Columbella Park?"

"It's catchy and appropriate."

"Except there aren't many Columbella shells on this coast." She waved the straw in his face. "See, the St. Regis family was crazy from the get-go."

He squished the drop of liquid that had dribbled from her straw onto the table. "For being such a crazy bunch, your ancestors sure amassed a ton of wealth."

The waiter appeared, parked a basket of steaming sweet potato fries on the table between them and took their order.

Dylan closed his eyes and inhaled the sweet scent. "Aah, this is the only reason I come to this place."

Mia stabbed one with her fork and blew on it.

Dylan's gaze lingered on her puckered lips. Those tasted sweeter than any sweet potato fries.

Shoving the basket toward him, Mia said, "You'd better eat the majority of those."

"Don't worry. I will." He dunked one of the fries in some ranch dressing. "Tell me about the plans for the park."

Mia outlined the restrictions and the hurdles she had to go through to complete the project. She talked about the park, and excitement lit her dark eyes until they sparkled. If only she didn't have the rest of the garbage hanging over her head. Momentarily freed from the burdens of the past few days, Mia smiled openly with no strain around her eyes. Unrestrained, her laugh gurgled from her throat.

And Dylan basked in her warm glow. It could be like this between them always. He needed her every bit as much as she thought she needed him.

One bite into his burger, his cell phone went off. He held up his index finger to stop Mia's conversation. "Hang on."

It was the station. "Reese."

"Chief, we have a fire just off the highway. Fire engines are on the way, but traffic's a mess."

"Any injuries?"

"Not that we know of."

"Give me the location. I'm in town, so it won't take me long to get there."

He ended the call and slipped the phone in the front pocket of his uniform. "Sorry, Mia. I have to run. Fire out on the highway."

"Let the firemen handle it."

"Uh, have you forgotten you're in Coral Cove? Police chief here is like a jack-of-all-trades." He tapped his plate of uneaten food. "Can you have them wrap this up and take it with you? I'll meet you at the Sea View when I'm done."

"I'll probably stay here and eat my salad."

He tugged her hair before tucking it behind her ear. "Drive carefully."

"You be careful. You're the one heading out to a fire."

Dropping some bills on the table, he scooted back his chair. "I'll give you a call."

She waved to him as he headed out the front door, and then settled back to eat her salad, trying to avoid the temptation of those fries.

"Excuse me?"

The waiter backtracked to the table, balancing three plates.

"Chief Reese had to leave. Could you please bring me a box for his food?"

"Sure thing. I heard about the fire out on the Coast Highway."

Nothing could remain a secret for long in a small town. Even if Jimmy Holt hadn't seen her paperwork for the park, everyone would've known about the park by tomorrow anyway.

She speared a piece of lettuce and cursed the sweet potato fry beckoning to her from the basket. Finally, the waiter dropped off a box and a bag. Mia loaded Dylan's burger into the box and dumped the rest of the fries on top of it, snatching one before closing the box.

She pinched the bill between two fingers, and her cell phone buzzed. Hope they weren't calling *her* to the fire. She glanced at the display, which read *Restricted*.

"Hello?"

"Ms. St. Regis? This is Kayla's nurse. Looks like Kayla's coming around. Thought you might want to be here."

Mia's heart raced and the blood in her veins sang. "Of course, I'll be right down."

Thank goodness the fire on the highway was north instead of south. She glanced at the bill and shoved it and Dylan's three twenties under the ketchup bottle for a generous tip and sprang from her chair.

She half-skipped, half-jogged to her car parked in a metered spot on Main Street beneath a streetlamp. No more back-alley parking spots where people could snip your brake lines unheeded.

She tossed her bag on the passenger seat, wedged the bag with Dylan's food against her purse and backed out of the parking spot. When she hit the turnoff for the highway, she could see billowing clouds of black smoke in the other direction, and the wind carried the pungent aroma of charred wood. Dylan would have his hands full, but he'd be thrilled when he found out Kayla had recovered.

Now she could tell them where she got those cookies. On the way to the hospital, Mia kept checking her phone, hoping the nurse wouldn't call back and tell her she'd been mistaken.

Mia's car rolled into the hospital parking lot, and she cruised up and down the first two aisles without finding a spot. This parking lot was always full.

She spotted a space near the end of one row and swung into it. She scrambled from her car, dragging her bag with her, and hitched it over her shoulder.

The warm breeze lifted the ends of her hair, and her low heels clicked on the asphalt as she maneuvered between the parked cars. Something rustled to her right. She paused. She scanned the dark parking lot. Her nostrils flared.

Swallowing hard, she made a beeline for the lighted hospital entrance. Out of the corner of her eye she saw a figure dart from behind a truck.

Adrenaline surged through her, and she spun to her right, arms outstretched. A masked person, completely outfitted in black, charged at her, a gleaming blade clutched in gloved hands.

A scream stuck in Mia's throat, and she clawed for the pepper spray Dylan had tucked into her bag. The bag slid from her shoulder and hit the ground, discharging its contents.

The stranger descended on her, wielding the knife in front of him. He slashed. She ducked. Never taking her eyes from the dark menace, she dropped to the ground and pawed through the items on the asphalt.

Curling her fingers around the pepper spray tube, she found her voice. She released the scream that had been gathering ever since the figure emerged from the darkness.

Then she wedged her thumb on to the button of the pepper spray. She swung her arm in front of her, the pepper spray clutched in her hand. She screamed again, and then growled, "Back off."

In the distance, she heard voices. "Hey, hey!"

The voices sounded so far away and the knife looked so close. The blade wavered for a moment and Mia jammed her thumb down on the pepper spray button.

The cylinder hissed, and the attacker staggered back, making another slashing motion toward Mia.

Mia gulped in some air and the taste of cayenne pepper flooded her mouth. She choked and dragged more air into her nose. Her nostrils caught fire and she fell backward.

Her eyes teared up and she choked. The knife came closer. She thrust her hands out...and waited for the first cut.

Chapter Fifteen

Dylan wiped the sweat and soot from his brow with his sleeve. Charred brush blew past him as he got in his car. Felt like the Santa Ana winds might be kicking up from L.A. It was a good thing the fire department got this blaze under control tonight before the winds really took off.

His stomach rumbled and his mouth watered when he thought about those sweet potato fries waiting for him. His mouth watered even more when he thought about the woman waiting for him.

He eased into the driver's seat and uncapped a bottle of water, courtesy of the Coral Cove Fire Department. He chugged half the bottle before coming up for air and reaching for his cell phone.

He punched the button for Mia's number and listened to the song playing on the other end. A man answered, and Dylan shot up in his seat. "Who's this?"

"Is this Chief Reese?"

Dylan's heart galloped in his chest, and he had

to peel his tongue from the roof of his dry mouth to answer. "Yeah, who the hell is this?"

"This is Dr. Chen at the Coral Cove Hospital. Ms. St. Regis had…an accident in our parking lot."

"What kind of accident?" And what had she been doing at the hospital when she was supposed to head straight back to the Sea View?

"Officer Baxter is already here. He was one of the only ones available because of the fire."

Officer Baxter? Why did they need a cop there for an accident? "Put him on."

"Hey, Chief."

"What the hell is going on out there, Baxter?"

"Ms. St. Regis was attacked in the hospital parking lot."

The blood pounded in Dylan's ears, and a bead of sweat trickled down the side of his face. "What kind of attack? Is she okay?"

"She's fine, a little choked up from the pepper spray."

Dylan threw his squad car into gear and peeled away from the shoulder of the highway. "Someone attacked her with pepper spray?"

"Ah, no. That was her own pepper spray—wind blew it back in her face. Someone attacked her with a knife."

"Good God!" Dylan almost swerved into oncoming traffic, and the blare of horns trailed after him as he straightened out his car. "Is she cut? Injured?"

"I told you, Chief, just a little choked up…and mad."

"Did you apprehend her attacker?"

"Nope. He got a little of the pepper spray and took off when a couple of emergency-room docs heard Ms. St. Regis scream in the parking lot."

"What was she doing at the hospital?"

"I couldn't tell you that, Chief."

"Let her know I'm on my way. Have you canvassed the area of the attack for any clues or evidence?"

"Palmer's doing that. We were the only two on-call with the fire going on."

Dylan's eyelid twitched. "Yeah, the fire."

"Anyone injured out there?"

"No. It was just a brush fire that closed the highway for an hour. I'm on my way."

Dylan ended the call and stepped on the accelerator. What the hell was Mia doing at the hospital, visiting Kayla? Jimmy Holt hadn't even published his article yet, and this crazy person had already set his sights on Mia.

She needed to get out of this town, and he planned to bundle her on the next flight out of San Francisco.

He cruised through the hospital parking lot, which now looked dark and sinister, and abandoned his squad car at the entrance. He careened around the corner to the emergency room and nodded at the front desk receptionist. "I'm looking for Mia St. Regis. One of my officers is with her."

"In the back, first door on your right."

She buzzed the doors for him and he crashed through. The first door to the right stood open, and a nurse, a doctor and Officer Baxter were all crowded around Mia, sitting on the edge of an examining table.

When she saw him at the door, she jumped from the table and wrapped herself around him. "I'm so glad you're here. Someone came at me with a knife, and I screamed and I pepper-sprayed him with the stuff you gave me, but the wind blew it back in my face, and you didn't warn me about that part."

"Shh." He smoothed the hair back from her forehead, and she peered at him through red-rimmed eyes. "Are you okay?"

"I am now." She burrowed her face against his chest.

"Is she okay, Doc?"

"Yes. She inhaled some of the pepper spray, but that will clear out of her system soon. That pepper spray probably saved her life, since she got her attacker, too."

"I don't know how much he suffered from the spray. He had a ski mask on, so he probably didn't breathe in any of the stuff. I think the emergency-room doctors scared him off."

"And your screaming." The doctor pressed some eye drops into Mia's hand. "Make sure you use these before you go to bed tonight. You should be fine tomorrow morning, and you're good to go home tonight."

Dylan turned to Baxter. "Has Palmer come back from the parking lot yet? I didn't see him out there."

"He didn't find anything, Chief. And as you heard from Ms. St. Regis, the perpetrator was disguised."

"Did he say anything to you, Mia?"

"No."

"What brought you out here?"

Coughing, she clamped her hands to her chest. "Kayla. I got a call from her nurse, or at least someone I thought was her nurse, telling me that Kayla had regained consciousness."

The blood in his veins chilled. Someone had lured her there, someone who knew how much she cared for her newfound niece. And the fire? Had someone set that fire to separate them?

"Kayla's nurse never called you?"

"No."

"Was it a woman who attacked you?"

"No. I don't know. The person seemed large."

"But it was definitely a woman on the phone?"

Mia's brow furrowed. "I think so. The voice was muffled, but I assumed it was Kayla's nurse."

"Do you have your phone?"

She pointed to the oversized bag hanging on the back of a chair. Dylan reached over and yanked it open. He felt inside and plucked out her cell. "Show me the call."

She pressed a key and held out the phone to him.

He squinted at the *restricted* message. "We can try to trace that call by having your carrier ping your phone."

"Do you really think the person would be dumb enough to call me from a traceable phone? You know as well as I do that number's going to go back to one of those temporary, throwaway phones or even a phone booth."

"You're probably right, but we'll give it a try anyway." He caught a tear trailing down her face.

"That's just from that horrible pepper spray." She blew her nose with a tissue. "And because Kayla's still in a coma."

"You're coming home with me again tonight."

The officer coughed and his cheeks reddened.

"Baxter, get out of here. I'll discuss this with you tomorrow. You on duty?"

"Yes, sir."

"Go home and get some sleep."

"You, too, sir."

Dylan glanced at the younger officer with narrowed eyes, but he'd turned away and exited the examination room.

"Are you ready?"

Mia nodded. "I just wanted to rip that ski mask off his face and ask him what he wanted. I don' understand any of it, Dylan. This much fanaticism over a house just doesn't make sense."

"Somebody's lost their mind. Just like that math teacher last summer."

She grimaced. "Yeah, another distant St. Regis relative."

As they left the hospital, Dylan slung his arm around her shoulders and pulled her flush with his body. "Could that be it? Some long-lost St. Regis relative?"

"The only long-lost St. Regis relative around here is Kayla. And look what happened to her."

An hour later, Mia snuggled against Dylan in his bed. When the masked man wielding the knife popped into her head, she closed her eyes and ran her hands across Dylan's smooth, warm flesh. The sensation made the nightmare recede.

But her actions made Dylan antsy.

The third time her hands fluttered across his flat belly, he grabbed them. "You're asking for trouble."

"Seems I don't even have to ask these days."

He rolled toward her and pressed the length of his body against hers, along every line. She had on another one of his T-shirts for pajamas, and the thin cotton only heightened the sensation as the cloth rubbed against every sensitive part of her body.

As he held her close, his heartbeat reverberated against her chest. The steady rhythm hypnotized her, soothed her until the masked man disappeared.

He murmured into her hair, "You're going home.

Coral Cove isn't safe for you, and nothing I can do can make it safe for you."

"I have to get Kayla settled first."

"Let me handle that. When her parents get here, they can take her home. She needs to be home with her parents right now, Mia, as much as you want her to be a substitute for Marissa."

Dylan knew her inside and out, every nook and cranny. "And my plans for the park?"

"Long distance. You already have the paperwork from Fielder. Teleconference, set up one of those online meetings. I'm sure he'll be happy to accommodate you."

"My sister?"

"You're not going to find her here. I'll handle that, too. We can treat her as a missing person, put out some bulletins."

"You have all the answers, don't you?"

He rubbed her back and she arched into his touch. "I try."

"What about us?"

His hand stilled. "I'm not letting you go, Mia. Not this time."

"You can't have it both ways, can you?" She flattened onto her back, away from his magic hands. "You can't send me away and hold on to me at the same time."

He tugged at the hem of her T-shirt and rolled it up her thighs. Didn't look like she could ever escape those magic hands. Didn't want to anyway.

"It won't be forever. Once you start demolishing the house, it's the end to whatever crazy plans this lunatic had for Columbella. It will be a done deal, not that I'll ever stop looking for the person who threatened you, harmed Kayla and killed Hank."

"You think it will ever be safe for me to return to Coral Cove?"

"Eventually. Hell, the guy could've made a mistake tonight. Maybe he left something in the parking lot, something we'll discover in the light of day."

"I hope it gets better. I want a real relationship with Kayla, away from all this drama. I want to get to know her as a person, not as a substitute for Marissa."

"I think you'll have that chance."

"Everything always seems better when I'm with you, Dylan. It always did."

He slid his hand beneath the T-shirt, and splayed it across her belly. "You should've asked me instead of Peter to marry you that summer."

She clenched her stomach. "I never wanted you like that, not through trickery. I always wanted you to come to me on your own. I waited."

He walked his fingers up between her breasts and cupped one in his hand. "You don't have to wait anymore."

Then he kissed her mouth and covered her body with his. No tricks. No schemes.

Dylan had come to her at last.

THE NEXT MORNING Mia woke up to the sound of the shower. She had to get going and set her plans in motion—all of her plans. She hated leaving Kayla, but Dylan was right. She needed her parents right now. She'd get in touch with the Rutherfords today and arrange to have Kayla airlifted to Arizona. Then she'd finalize some of the forms Dirk had given her to convert Columbella into a park. Last on her list was getting a flight back to New York. After the night she and Dylan had shared, her fears about leaving him seemed ridiculous. They belonged together. Why hadn't they realized that sooner?

But the years apart had made them an even better fit. Dylan had been too perfect for her, had taken himself too seriously. She was sorry for his experience with the Lords and Melody's death, but it had made him realize that people were flawed. She was flawed. That judgmental side of him that had always scared her off had mellowed.

She'd learned from her mistakes, too. Life was not one big joke. Some games had consequences.

The bathroom door opened with a whoosh of lemon-scented steam and Dylan emerged with a towel wrapped around his waist. "Did I wake you?"

She stretched and swung her legs over the side of the bed. "Yes, but I need to get up. I have a busy day ahead of me."

"Which includes getting on a flight to New York."

"Realistically, I don't think that's going to happen today, but maybe tomorrow."

"That will give me a chance to take the day off work tomorrow and drive you up to San Francisco."

Planting her feet on the floor, she said, "You don't have to drive me up to the city."

"Yeah, I do." He ran a hand through his wet hair, and it curled at the ends. "Leave your rental car at the same office where you got the replacement, and I'll drop you off at the airport."

"You have to work today, and I have to get some stuff done."

"Just tell me where you're headed at all times, and I'll arrange to have someone tail you."

"You're going to get in trouble using the Coral Cove police force as a private security agency."

"Nobody has to go out of his or her way. It's a small town. What are your plans?"

She held up her hand and ticked off her fingers. "I'm going to the hospital to visit Kayla and set up air transport to take her to Arizona. I have to drop by City Hall and turn some forms over to Dirk. I'd like to go back out to Columbella and finish my inventory. I can't trash the entire interior. There are some one-of-a-kind items out there."

Dylan twisted his lips. "That's all doable, but I don't like the idea of you out at Columbella again."

"You can send me with a police escort." She waved her hand. "I'll be fine."

"Maybe I should teach you how to use that pepper spray."

She cleared her throat, which still burned. "I did use it correctly. The wind blew it back in my face."

"You have to angle away from any breeze."

"Yeah, like that's what I was thinking when confronted with that knife-wielding maniac."

He strolled to his dresser and pulled out a pair of boxers. Keeping his towel in place as if she hadn't already seen it all before, he struggled into his boxers.

"Nothing about the stranger seemed familiar? The way he moved, carried himself, shoes?"

"I guess I'd make a terrible witness, but all I saw was the knife."

"That's really common. Once someone pulls out a weapon, that's all the victim notices."

She straightened her shoulders and marched to the bathroom. "I am not a victim."

Later that morning, true to his word, Dylan followed her back to the Sea View and waited while she changed clothes. Then he followed her back to town and joined her on the sidewalk in front of City Hall.

He reached around her and plucked a newspaper from the stack in the wooden kiosk. He held it up in front of his chest, and Mia read aloud, 'Demolition for Columbella House.'

She smacked the paper. "Oh, that's not sensational at all."

Dylan turned the paper around. "At least he added the bit about the park beneath the headline."

"So neither side is going to be happy with me."

"Ha! When did that ever bother a St. Regis? *Regis* means 'king,' right? The St. Regises have always been masters of their own destinies."

She jerked her thumb over her shoulder. "Okay, I'm going to meet with Dirk right now. It should take me a few hours if you're keeping tabs."

"I'm keeping tabs." He folded the paper and handed it to her. "Let me know when you're done with Dirk. Hospital after?"

"Yes, I called earlier. No change for Kayla, but she's not any worse and there's definitely no damage to her organs."

"That's good news. Before you know it, you'll be visiting her in Arizona, or a more likely scenario is she'll be hitting you up for a place to stay in New York."

"She won't have to hit me up." Mia tucked the paper into her bag. "She'll be a wealthy young woman in her own right."

"Don't overwhelm her, Mia. Sometimes riches don't do anyone any good."

"And sometimes they do a lot of good, like right now. I'm going to arrange air transport for her with a nurse onboard."

He kissed the top of her head. "Sounds like a good use for your dough. Keep me posted. I'm going to get you out of this town tomorrow."

He waited in his squad car at the curb until she entered the building.

Dirk rose from his chair when she walked into his office. "Whew, I thought you were going to keep this plan under wraps. Since the *Coral Cove Herald* hit the stands, my phone's been ringing nonstop."

"That intrepid reporter, Jimmy Holt, got hold of the story and ran with it. Are the calls positive or negative?"

"About half and half, which just goes to show you, you can't please all the people all the time."

She dropped a stack of papers on his desk. "Let's go through what I need to sign, since I'm leaving for New York tomorrow."

"So soon?" He frowned and spun the stack around to face him. "I guess we can do a lot of this long-distance."

"It's not safe for me here. Someone is a little too invested in the fate of Columbella. I was attacked last night in the hospital parking lot."

Dirk drew his glasses to the tip of his nose and peered over the top. "Are you kidding?"

"Deadly serious. I think the same person might be behind the poisoning of my niece."

"That's nuts. Then that same person killed Hank the homeless guy?"

"Exactly."

"The chief better get on the ball then. Our previous chief had a lackadaisical air about serious crime in this town, and we gave him the boot."

"I thought he took a job elsewhere."

"He took a job elsewhere because he was so unpopular here." Dirk thumbed through the forms and pulled one from the stack. "Sign here, too."

She snatched a pen from the holder shaped like a fish and scribbled her name on the line where he was tapping his finger.

He slid open a file drawer to his left and pulled out another form. "You need to sign this."

Mia scanned the form while Dirk tapped his pen on his desk blotter. "The mayor should be happy about this," he said.

"Tyler? I thought he and his wife were in the renovation camp."

"They are, but he'd like to see more parks in Coral Cove. He mentioned it to me once when he talked about what he'd do if the house ever came to the city."

"Why would the house go to the city?" Mia bit the end of the pen and squinted at the small print on the form.

"I hope you're reading these forms better than you apparently read your grandfather's will."

She jerked up her head. "Huh?"

"In the event of your death and no other direct St Regis descendants, which means offspring belonging to you or Marissa, Columbella House goes to the city. I've seen the documents."

"Really?" Mia initialed the bottom of the page and flipped it over. "But Tyler wants it to be a park?"

"He mentioned something like that."

Mia signed the back of the form and slid it across the table. Dylan had asked her who got the house if she died an untimely death. If the city got it, that wouldn't do one person any good, would it?

She spent the next hour and a half with Dirk and left him with her email address and all possible phone numbers.

He walked her into the hallway where Tyler was just coming out of his office.

He saluted. "Hey, Mia, are you finalizing the deal to turn Columbella House into a park?"

"Not quite final yet, Mayor, but the wheels are turning." She tilted her head toward Dirk. "The city planner here told me you were interested in turning Columbella into a park."

"More greenbelt for a city is always good." He turned to Dirk. "Can I have a minute, Dirk?"

"Sure. We just finished."

The two propped up the wall while they put their heads together, and Mia pulled out her phone and pressed the key for Dylan's cell.

"Okay, Chief. I'm done at City Hall and I'm going to head over to the hospital."

"Are you satisfied now that you can do *everything* long- distance?"

She whispered into the phone. "We can't do *everything* long-distance."

He chuckled. "I meant the plans for Columbella House."

"Oh, that. Yeah, we'll get it done."

"Good. Don't leave City Hall until you see a squad car coming down the street. Officer Baxter is on patrol today, and he could use a run down the highway to the hospital."

"Got it. I feel like the queen or something."

"You're *my* queen, babe."

Another little piece of her heart melted. "I'll call you after my next stop."

She waved to Dirk and Tyler and stationed herself on the sidewalk. Two minutes later, a police car rolled around the corner. She held up her hand and made for her car. She tossed her bundle of papers in the backseat, snapped her seat belt and pulled away from the curb, the patrol car tailing her to the highway.

Fifteen minutes later when she cruised into the hospital parking lot, a chill snaked through her body. Dylan had sent an officer over this morning to see if she could find any more evidence at the scene of the attack. Since he hadn't mentioned a word about it over the phone, Mia assumed the cop hadn't discovered anything new.

She parked and Officer Baxter remained right beside her, his engine idling. He crawled behind her until she got to the hospital doors. Leave it to Dylan to put a twenty-four-hour watch on her.

She took a deep breath and closed her eyes. *Happy thoughts. Happy thoughts.*

She went up to the third floor and stopped by the nurses' station. "I'm back. How's she doing?"

Geri came from the back, carrying a tray with pills on it. "I'm so sorry about last night. That's just creepy that someone would use my name to lure you out here and attack you."

"It's not your fault. The person on the phone didn't even give her name. I just assumed it was you. I guess I was so anxious for good news about Kayla."

She set down the tray. "She's doing well. She stirred a little bit this morning." She glanced over her shoulder and held her finger to her lips. "Don't tell Dr. Fitzwilliam I said this, but I think she's going to come out of this soon."

"I hope so, but I have to go back to New York tomorrow. I'm making arrangements to have her taken to Phoenix by helicopter."

"Oh, you're going to deny us the pleasure of being with her when she wakes up?"

"Her parents are in Phoenix. They're worried sick."

"You're a good aunt, Mia, and I think it's great what you're doing with that creepy old house. Even a restoration won't get rid of the ghosts out there."

"You think there are ghosts?"

"Absolutely."

"Well, hopefully they won't haunt the park."

"They'll disappear once you demolish the old place. Maybe all the spirits will escape out to sea."

Mia raised her brows. Nurse Geri must've been a good customer of Rosie the fortune-teller.

"Let's hope everyone is as happy as you to see that house and land become a park. Can I see Kayla now?"

"Go right in. I'll send Dr. Fitzwilliam by when he gets a moment so you can discuss her needs with him and give him the Phoenix hospital info."

Mia walked down the corridor and pushed open the door to Kayla's private room. The flowers she'd brought the day before emitted a luscious scent that blotted out the antiseptic hospital smell.

"Good news, Kayla." Mia dragged a chair to the side of the bed. "You're going home to your parents."

She smoothed her hand across Kayla's cool forehead. "But you're not getting rid of me that easily. I'll be keeping tabs on you, and I'll pay for your college. I'll buy you that car. I'll do everything my sister would've done for you. She'd be the perfect mom for a teenage girl. Because wherever she is, I'm sure she never grew up."

Mia's voice caught and she covered her mouth, turning away. She had to stay positive for Kayla.

"Your friends are still here, too. They'll come

and visit you when they get back to Phoenix. They're going to cut their road trip short."

Amid Kayla's steady breaths, she released a soft sigh.

Mia's heart jumped and she scooted her chair closer to the bed. "Kayla? Can you hear me?"

Kayla's lashes stirred on her cheeks, and another sigh escaped her lips.

Mia jumped from her chair and it clattered to the floor. She tripped to the door and gripped the doorjamb as she arched into the hallway. "Nurse, nurse! Dr. Fitzwilliam!"

Nurse Geri strode down the hallway, her sneakers squeaking on the floor. "What is it?"

"It's Kayla. She's stirring. She made a couple of noises. She almost opened her eyes."

Geri brushed past her and picked up Kayla's wrist. Then she hunched over her patient and pushed up one of her eyelids, shining a small penlight into her eye.

"Looks good. I'm going to get Dr. Fitzwilliam. Keep talking to her." She hurried from the room.

Mia righted the chair and drummed her fingers on Kayla's arm. "Keep it up, kid. We're all waiting for you on the other side."

Dr. Fitzwilliam bustled into the room. "Ms. St. Regis, I'd like to start running a few tests. You can leave now. I'll give you a call."

Mia backed out of the room, sending a silent prayer in Kayla's direction. Maybe Kayla could fly home to Phoenix and walk off the plane on her own.

Maybe she could tell Dylan who gave her the cookies, and Mia could feel safe again in her hometown.

Slumping in a chair in the hospital lobby, Mia pulled out her cell phone and called Dylan. He seemed out of breath when he answered. "Busy day?"

"You could say that. Now the mayor wants a meeting with me this afternoon."

"You know I found out from Dirk Fielder that he city gets the house if I die. So no one person would benefit from that."

"That's interesting—good to know. You're still at the hospital?"

"I am, and I have some good news. Kayla is showing some signs of life. She made some noises and she moved her eyelids. Dr. Fitzwilliam is running some tests right now."

"That's great news. What about the transport back to Arizona?"

"It's all set to go, but I'm sure Dr. Fitzwilliam will want to keep her here if she keeps showing igns of improvement. I can fly Mr. and Mrs. Ruthrford out here instead. If I'm still leaving tomorrow, I want someone out here for Kayla."

"You *are* still leaving tomorrow, bright and early, and I'll look after Kayla until her parents get here. Her friends are still in town, too."

"All right, all right. I know you're not budging on that."

"Where are you headed now?"

"Is it okay if I have lunch?"

"Wish I could join you but duty calls. Where are you going?"

"I think I might just have to go back to the Whole Earth Café and have some of those sweet potato fries."

"Don't leave the hospital until you see Baxter in the parking lot."

Mia crossed her legs at the ankles and tapped her sandals together. "Isn't he getting a little tired of shadowing me today?"

"Are you kidding? He'd rather be driving around town than pulling over kids on bikes for not wearing helmets or settling some domestic dispute."

"Well, then send him on over. I'm starving."

Mia watched for the familiar black-and-white squad car out the window. When Baxter pulled up to the curb, she exited the hospital and waved to him on her way to her car.

He followed her back to Main Street, and Mia sauntered to his car after she parked in a metered space on the street. He powered down the window at her approach.

"I'm grabbing a bite to eat at the Whole Earth. Do you want something?"

"No, thank you, Ms. St. Regis. I'm meeting my girlfriend for a sandwich in the park."

"Aww, that's sweet." She gestured toward the restaurant. "I'm sure Chief Reese will be letting you know your next assignment after lunch. Sorry."

"No need to apologize. This is an easy gig for me today."

He watched her walk into the restaurant and then took off for his own rendezvous.

Mia surveyed the crowded restaurant for a friendly face but got a few blank stares and sideways glances in response. Everyone must've read the article by now. Didn't anyone want a park?

"Table for one?" The hostess smiled sweetly but Mia saw signs of pity on her face.

"Yep, that's me, dining solo."

The hostess led her to a table by the kitchen. After Mia sat down, she pulled the *Coral Cove Herald* out of her bag. She shook out the paper and read the front-page article. Holt had made it sound like she was tearing down some beloved gathering place instead of the town eyesore and local haunted house.

He sure knew how to whip up negative public opinion. Maybe *he* had some stake in keeping the drama swirling around the house.

The waiter stopped by her table almost as an afterthought, and Mia ordered the sweet potato fries along with a diet soda—had to balance out those calories somehow.

When her order came, she folded the paper and

stuffed it back in her bag. She dragged the basket of fries in front of her and plunged in.

"To die for, aren't they?"

Mia glanced up at Linda Davis, all gussied up in a pink suit and hovering near her table.

"They are heavenly." She jabbed a fry in Linda's direction. "You look nice."

"Thanks. Showing a house later." She placed a hand on the chair across from Mia. "Mind if I join you? The place is packed."

Mia scanned the crowded room, buzzing with activity. "Sure, if you don't mind the noise from the kitchen."

"Not at all." She pulled out the chair, waved down the waiter and ordered a sandwich and an iced tea, which was delivered seconds after she sat down.

"Does the mayor's wife always get such quick service? I swear that waiter has been hard to find since I sat down."

Linda rolled her eyes. "One of the small perks, the very small perks. Maybe you'll find out when you're the police chief's wife."

Mia brushed her fingers together and took a sip of her soda. "Is that the buzz in town?"

"That and your plans for the park."

"Oh, you saw that, huh?"

"You'd have to be living under a rock not to."

"I hope you don't mind too much, Linda. I know we discussed the renovation and you went to a lot of trouble the other day helping me with the inventory."

She fluttered her manicured fingers. "Don't even think about it. I was happy to have a look around, and Tyler is thrilled with the park idea."

"Good. I'm actually headed over there after lunch to finish up the inventory. I'm going to strip the place before I have it demolished."

Linda had been dumping a pack of sweetener in her iced tea and she dropped the little blue envelope in her tea. She fished it out with her spoon. "I'd love to join you. I'm heading that way for my listing on Coral Cove Drive."

"Perfect. I just have to let my police bodyguard know where I'm going next."

"Your police bodyguard?"

Mia held a finger to her lips. "Shh, don't tell your husband. Noah Baxter is on patrol, and Dylan keeps sending him to follow me from place to place."

"I didn't see a black-and-white out front."

"Oh, he just escorts me to my location and then takes off until I'm done. He's having lunch in the park with his girlfriend right now."

Linda thanked the waiter for her sandwich and began slicing off the crusts with a knife. "And why exactly do you need a bodyguard? Because of that rock thrown at you during the protest?"

Mia waved to get the waiter's attention for a refill on her soda and gave up. "I guess news doesn't travel as fast as I thought it did in a small town.

I was attacked last night in the parking lot of the hospital."

Linda's eyes widened and her lip twitched. "Oh, my God. Are you okay?"

"I'm fine, but Dylan wants me under lock and key before I take off tomorrow. I'm surprised Tyler didn't tell you. He seems to have his pulse on everything that happens."

"I didn't see my husband this morning, and you must know the new chief doesn't keep the mayor as informed as much as the previous chief did."

"Yeah, Dylan likes his independence."

"A man like Dylan Reese will never be controlled."

"Oh, I know that, and I'm okay with it." Mia hid her smile behind her napkin. No wonder Tyler liked to flex his muscles as mayor. He probably didn't get the opportunity at home.

Linda took a delicate bite of her sandwich and dabbed her lips with a napkin. "I hope you're carrying some kind of protection. A girl can't be too careful, even in a small town like this."

"I have some pepper spray. That's how I got away last night."

Linda patted her bag. "I keep a small gun with me at all times."

"Really?"

"Just started this summer when we had that serial killer on the loose." She tapped Mia's empty glass. "Are you ready to go over now?"

"First I need to activate my bodyguard service." She dug her cell phone from her purse and called Dylan. "I'm heading over to Columbella House now."

"Okay, I'll get Baxter over to meet you at the restaurant. I can't talk now. I've got a busy afternoon."

"Don't worry. I'll have company at the house." She winked at Linda.

"I'll get Baxter on the radio. Take care."

Mia crumpled her napkin and dropped it on the table. "My police escort is on his way."

"Does that mean you're done with these?" Linda held up the basket of fries.

"Knock yourself out. Now if I can just get that waiter to bring me my check."

"Don't worry about it. I'll pick it up."

"Thanks. Let me know what I owe you when you get to the house." Mia slung her bag over her shoulder and left the restaurant. Poor Noah wasn't there yet, probably still enjoying lunch with his girlfriend.

Mia leaned against her car and called the hospital. Kayla had made a few signs that she was coming out of her coma, but the doctor hadn't finished his tests yet. If Kayla could identify the person who gave her the cookies, Mia wouldn't have to rush out of town.

She didn't want to leave Dylan—not now, not ever.

Noah's car cruised to a stop in front of the Whole

Earth, and Mia waved and slid into her car. On the way to Columbella, Dylan called.

"Baxter's there?"

"Right behind me."

"I don't like the idea of you shuffling around that old house by yourself. I can't ask Baxter to stay because he needs to be on patrol."

"Don't worry. I told you. I'm going to have company. I'm meeting Linda Davis there—and she carries a gun. Did you know that?"

"I knew she had a conceal-and-carry permit. Just don't open the door to anyone, and maybe by the time you're done I'll be off and I'll give you my own private escort."

"Mmm, that sounds good. Kayla continues to make progress."

"That's good to hear. I gotta go. You have a meeting with the mayor's wife and I have a meeting with the mayor."

They ended the call just about the time Mia turned off the highway. She passed the house for sale with Linda's sign out front and then pulled into the driveway of Columbella—maybe for the last time.

Noah idled at the curb and Mia approached the car. "I think you're good to go, Noah."

"The chief told me to wait until Mrs. Davis shows up."

Mia pointed to Linda's black Mercedes pulling

in front of the house for sale. "She just did. Thanks for your help today."

He took off, and Mia picked her way up the walk. Linda waved from across the street and pointed to her listing. Probably had a few things to do there first to get ready for her showing later.

Mia's key slid easily into the new lock and she stepped into the foyer. She breathed in the musty smell of the house and sneezed. No amount of renovation could make this place right again.

For the next twenty minutes she wandered around the house, taking notes of the pieces. Columbella was still a treasure trove.

The knock on the front door startled her into dropping her notepad. She rushed to the front window and peered out. Linda stood out like a pink marshmallow on the dreary porch.

Mia opened the door and ushered her in. "You should've changed into something grungier."

"I don't mind getting a little dirty."

"I tallied a few more items." She held out the notepad to Linda. "Maybe I should have an estate sale or something before the teardown."

"If you're talking estate sale, we need to go through that basement."

Mia wrapped her arms around herself and shivered. "I hate it down there."

"It'll be okay with the two of us." Linda reached into her purse and withdrew a dull gray handgun. "The three of us."

For some reason, the sight of the gun sent more chills racing down Mia's back. "Y-you know how to use that thing, right?"

"I sure do."

On unsteady legs, Mia led the way to the basement door. She pushed it open and flicked on the lights. She descended a few steps and cranked her head over her shoulder.

"These steps are not the safest."

Linda placed a hand on her back, and at first Mia thought she had stumbled. "Be careful."

"No, you be careful." Linda gave her a hard shove down the stairs.

Chapter Sixteen

Dylan sat in the mayor's office, tapping his foot. Mayor Davis had called this meeting and he couldn't make it on time? He glanced at his watch again. Baxter had touched base to let him know Mia was at Columbella with Linda Davis…and Linda had a gun.

Hope she knew how to use it better than Mia knew how to use that pepper spray.

He eased back in the comfortable leather chair and propped his feet on the mayor's desk, littered with pictures of him and his wife. The two had never had children.

His gaze scanned the photos—all vacation pictures. Mia had mentioned the two traveled every summer, usually to some exotic locale, although they'd had to skip this summer because of all the trouble.

Dylan zeroed in on one picture, a shot of Linda with an expanse of beach and blue sea behind her. He sat up and reached for the photo. The place looked familiar. A white, domed building gleamed in the background. Where had he seen that building?

His heart banged against his rib cage. *Marissa's postcards.*

He scrambled to the other side of the desk and hunched over the photos, picking up each one and holding it close to his face. This could be Cote d'Azur, this could be the Costa del Sol, this could be Nice with that lighthouse in the distance. The same lighthouse on Marissa's postcard.

Dylan dropped the last frame and it clattered on the mayor's desk. What did it mean? Had the Davises been sending Mia phony postcards from Marissa all these years? And if so, why?

He didn't have time to hang around here and ask Mayor Davis. Mia was at Columbella alone with Linda Davis…and Linda had a gun.

He lunged for the door and ran across the old linoleum floor of City Hall. He burst out the front, nearly knocking over the city treasurer. He gunned his squad car and raced out the back way, but didn't flip on his siren. He wanted to take Linda by surprise—if there was any reason to take her by surprise.

All those trips could just be a coincidence. But the city got the house if Mia died. Mayor Tyler Davis *was* the city. What it all had to do with Marissa and those postcards he didn't know, but he planned to find out.

He left his car around the corner from Columbella House. Mia had parked her car in the driveway, and Linda had left her car at the curb in front of the house for sale.

He tried the front door, and wasn't surprised it was locked. Cupping his hands around his face, he peered into the windows, but nothing stirred amid the shrouded furniture.

If he rang the bell and made his presence known, what would Linda do? She couldn't shoot Mia with him standing on the porch and hope to get away with it.

But he didn't want to test his theory.

He crept around the side of the house and peeled back the plywood over the kitchen window. He unlocked the door from within and eased it open.

He stood inside, cocking his head, listening for voices. The house creaked in response. He moved on silent feet across the floor and froze.

A muffled scream came from somewhere below. The basement. He sidled along the wall until he reached the basement door. Pressing his ear against the wood, he turned the knob. The handle turned but something else barred the door—deadbolt?

If he shot through it now, there was no telling what he'd hit on the other side. He had to get in another way—through the beach entrance.

He backed away from the door and whispered, "Hang on, Mia."

He half slid, half ran down the trail to the beach,

banging his knees on more than a few rocks on his way down. He circled around the sea cave and made his way along the cement path that led to the basement door of Columbella.

The lock had been broken for years, and he held his breath as he inched open the door. The small movement must've caught Mia's eye as she sat on the bottom step of the staircase, facing him.

She was holding her arm, and her face was bleeding. Rage clawed through him as his gaze tracked to Linda, pointing a gun at Mia's head.

Mia's eyes seemed to lock on to his for a moment. He held a finger to his lips before her gaze flicked away. He didn't have a clue how he was going to open the rest of this door without Linda hearing him in the silence of the basement.

And then the basement was no longer silent.

Mia screamed again and pushed over a drum kit in the corner before scrambling for the stairs. Amid the clash of cymbals and the rolling of a big bass drum, Dylan pushed through the door and crouched behind a pile of inner tubes and tires.

Linda caught Mia's ankle and yanked her back down the stairs. "What's the matter with you? I thought you wanted to hear what happened to Marissa. You'll never find out if you make me kill you now."

Mia resumed her seat on the bottom step, rubbing her knees. "I do want to find out what you did to Marissa."

"I didn't do anything to Marissa. Tyler killed her."

Mia gasped, and then tears flooded her eyes. Marissa. Marissa was dead.

Linda laughed. "Yeah, I know, right? Didn't expect that out of him. Of course, he screwed it up, as usual.

"It really was your fault, Mia. You brought that Brazilian god back here, and Marissa couldn't resist him. I think she still planned to go through with a marriage to Tyler, though—slut. She wanted a little fun on the side, and then figured she'd settle down with Tyler and swipe this house from right under your nose."

Mia rubbed her eyes. "Is that the reason Tyler wanted to marry her, too? To get this house?"

"This house and all the millions and power that came with the St. Regis name, but he really did love your sister—the idiot."

"Then why did he k-kill her?"

"Why did he k-kill her? Jealousy. He caught her with the Brazilian. He'd been spying on them. He offered the man money to get out of town, and he took it. Real gem you had there, Mia."

"If Raoul had already agreed to leave town, why did Tyler kill Marissa?"

Linda still had the gun pointed at her. Could Dylan shoot now and take her out? She didn't want him to, not yet. She had to hear what had happened to Marissa.

"She laughed at him." Linda wagged her finger. "Never laugh at a man, Mia, even a milquetoast like Tyler. Your sister told Tyler that she expected an open marriage. She wanted her dalliances with men like Raoul, but she and Tyler could present a united front to the town. You St. Regis women and your marriages of convenience."

"So Tyler killed her in a jealous rage?"

"That's right."

"Did he throw her body into the ocean? Weigh it down?" Mia clamped her trembling hands between her knees. Could she handle this?

"No." An evil gleam lighted Linda's eyes. "Don't you remember Charlie Vega had put in the cement flooring in here?"

Mia nodded, a sour lump forming in her throat.

Linda pointed to a spot on the cement floor of the basement. "She's right there."

Sobbing, Mia doubled over. All this time. Kylie Grant had been right. She must've sensed Marissa's presence in the house.

She shuddered and jerked up her head. "That's why you don't want me to tear down the house. As soon as this floor is ripped up, they'll find Marissa."

"We wanted you to renovate. We could've covered up then."

"How did you know Tyler murdered her?"

Linda clapped her hands. "I witnessed it. I used it to get him to marry me. Marissa St. Regis didn't need the Davis name in this town, but poor little Linda Gruber from the wrong side of the tracks did."

"You wanted to marry him after that? And protect him?"

"Whatever he had became mine, so of course I wanted to protect it."

"But even if Marissa's…remains were discovered, why would anyone suspect Tyler? Everyone might have suspected Raoul."

"I told you Tyler screwed up, didn't I?" The gun wavered for a moment and Mia shot a quick glance at Dylan, still ensconced behind the tires and inner tubes.

"I'd say he screwed up the moment he killed my sister."

Linda snorted. "The idiot dropped his watch in the cement, the watch your sister gave him on their engagement. Pretty incriminating, wouldn't you say?"

"So ever since I've been back, you've been trying to get me out of the way to get your hands on the house. The city would get the house and Tyler could influence its fate."

"That's right, Mia—the brakes on your car, the stupid doll—that was Tyler's idea, too. He's full of dumb ideas. And he screwed up the attack on you in the hospital parking lot. Doesn't really have the stomach for murder anymore."

"Peter?"

She shrugged, and the gun bobbed again. "He was threatening to sue you for the house. He would've held things up. You didn't like him anyway, so I pushed him off the cliff for you. Where's the thanks?"

Mia's stomach twisted into knots. "And Kayla?"

"That was a surprise out of left field. Told you Marissa was a slut."

"Did you give her those cookies?"

"Tyler and I were at that little gathering the Vegas had after their big blowout on Main Street. When your niece left the house, I ran after her with the bag of cookies, which I'd actually baked for you. Told her Tina wanted her to have them."

"She'll tell us that when she comes to."

"Well, we never expected or wanted her to survive. Another Tyler screwup. He didn't put in enough poison. One cookie should've been enough."

"Two were enough for Hank."

"Hank was the town drunk. What do you expect? Kayla was young and healthy."

"Kayla *is* young and healthy. She's coming out of her coma." Mia licked her lips. She had to somehow get out of Linda's range to give Dylan a chance to disarm her. "When she does, she's going to explain how you ran after her with the cookies."

Linda bit her lip and then shrugged. "I'll figure out something. I did manage to pull off Marissa's disappearance, and now you're going to disappear just like your twin."

Mia braced her hands against the step, raising herself an inch. Her triceps tensed, her eyes never leaving the barrel of the gun.

"I'm not shooting you, Mia—too much blood, too much noise. Get up."

Linda raised the gun and Mia saw her chance. She launched herself toward Linda's legs. Linda staggered, but dug her pink heels into the basement floor. Grabbing the gun with both hands, she brought it down toward Mia's head.

A shot blasted out, the sound deafening in the enclosed space. Linda's grip on the gun loosened, and Mia rolled out of her range. Then Linda's gun followed Mia's path, and another shot cracked through the basement.

This time Linda pitched forward, her forehead smacking against the cement—right where Tyler had buried Marissa.

From the floor, Mia looked up at Dylan, his weapon still raised in front of him, his mouth a thin line, his eyes deadly.

Mia crawled away from the pool of blood oozing from the back of Linda's head. Then she collapsed on the floor, her hands splayed against the cement that encased her sister's remains.

Dylan swooped down and picked her up in his arms. "You're hurt. How did she hurt you?"

Mia shook her head. "It doesn't matter, none of it matters. Marissa's dead, has been dead for years."

"Shh, I know." He moved toward the stairs, punched in 911 and gave the operator the basics.

The basement door above them splintered under a heavy assault. Dylan spun around, training his gun on the intruder.

Tyler Davis cried out and stumbled down the stairs. "Linda!"

"Hold it right there, Davis."

Tyler, his gaze focused on his dead wife, ignored the warning as he continued his descent.

Dylan kicked Linda's gun under the stairs.

When Tyler reached the bottom of the stairs, he flung himself onto Linda's body, sobbing and shaking. "Linda, Linda, Linda. I told you not to come here today."

"It's over, Davis. She confessed everything. We know that you killed Marissa St. Regis and tried to kill Mia and her niece. We know you're responsible for Hank's death and Peter's."

Tyler didn't respond. He pulled his wife's bloody head against his chest and smoothed her sticky hair from her forehead. "We'll get through this, Linda. I'll get us through this time."

When the cops arrived, they had to pry Tyler from Linda. True devotion to the very end.

Dylan stuck by Mia's side through the whole ruckus. When the cops had taken Tyler away and the EMTs had loaded Linda's body into the ambulance, Mia finally closed her eyes.

"How did you know, Dylan? How did you figure out Linda was a threat?"

He pulled her close. "The pictures in Tyler's office, all those vacation photos—from all the places in Marissa'a postcards."

Mia shook her head. "It was all so pointless."

"I'm sorry, Mia. I hope you can stop blaming yourself now for Marissa's fate."

"Linda tried to put the blame on me, but I'm not buying it. She and Tyler orchestrated this whole outrage from beginning to end. She had an opportunity to turn in Tyler after witnessing him kill my sister, but instead she chose to exploit the situation for her own gain."

"It's over. It's finally over. Maybe the curse of Columbella House can finally be laid to rest."

Mia buried her head against his chest as the sun began its descent into the ocean. "The curse didn't start with Marissa's murder and it's not going to end with the discovery of her body. I'm doing the right thing by destroying this house. Maybe then the curse can be laid to rest for good."

Epilogue

Mia held Dylan's hand and gazed at the expanse of green grass rolling to the cliff's edge. The roof of the gazebo sparkled in the sun, and the ocean breeze carried the sound of children's laughter.

She sighed. "Perfect timing for the completion of the park with school ending this week."

Michelle Girard strolled toward them, Colin Roarke's arm encircling her waist. "Hello, Mia. The park is beautiful. Colin and I were thinking it would make a great place for a wedding."

Mia tilted her head. "Anyone's wedding in particular?"

Michelle's cheeks turned pink as Colin hugged her close. Colin laughed and said, "Ours, of course."

Michael Roarke strode up to his uncle and jutted out his lower lip. "Uncle Colin, weddings are yucky."

Colin ruffled his hair. "We'll try to make ours as un-yucky as possible because you're going to have to be in it."

Michael stuck out his tongue and tugged on Dylan's sleeve. "Uncle Dylan, you're not going to get married, are you? And if you do, I'm not going to be in it, am I?"

Dylan's sister, Devon, strolled up to the group arm-in-arm with her husband and Colin's brother, Kieran. "That's not very nice, Michael. If Uncle Dylan wants you in his wedding, you're going to be in his wedding."

Michael's mouth dropped open. "You mean you're getting married, too?"

Kieran scooped up his son and hoisted him to his shoulders. "Hey, what's wrong with getting married? Your mom and I are married and if we weren't, you wouldn't be here."

Michael scrunched up his face. "Hmm, does that mean I might get some cousins out of this? Because Luke McBain at school is always bragging about all the stupid cousins he has, and I don't have any. Do I, Mom?"

Devon pinched her brother's waist and winked at Colin. "Not yet."

The engine of a Harley cut through the pleasant sounds of the afternoon, and Dylan's friend Matt Conner cruised to a stop in the park's small parking lot. He helped his girlfriend, Kylie Grant, off the bike, and his black motorcycle boots crunched the gravel on the winding path.

"Hey, Chief Reese, don't you have a town to protect?"

The men gave each other a one-armed hug and Mia stood on tiptoes to kiss Matt's cheek. She whispered, "Thanks so much for all your help."

"Dylan did all the hard work. I'm just sorry it ended like it did."

Kylie took Mia's hand. "And I'm sorry my prediction came true. I struggled with telling you."

"I'm glad you did."

Michelle touched Mia's shoulder. "I have something for you. Hold out your hand."

Mia held out her hand, and Michelle poured a charm bracelet into her palm. Mia hung the bracelet from her finger and dangled it in the sunshine. Tears sprang to her eyes. "It's Marissa's, the one you found at Columbella."

Michelle nodded. "My mother made it for her. Actually, Colin found it in the basement of Columbella."

Devon joined the circle of women. "Did Davis ever return Marissa's diary that Kieran and I found at Columbella? Dylan told me Tyler admitted taking a shot at me that night and then stealing the diary."

"Tyler gave it to me. He had it with him in prison and asked me to visit him there. He apologized for everything and handed me the diary."

"The mayor's actions when Matt and I were searching for that other missing woman, Bree Harris, make total sense now." The breeze lifted Kylie's long black hair, and she caught it with one hand. "He didn't want anyone searching around that house."

"Aunt Mia!"

Mia swung around and waved at the pretty girl sprinting across the grass.

Devon whistled. "Oh, my God, she looks exactly like Marissa. You're going to have your hands full with that one."

Kayla launched herself at Mia and gave her a bear hug. "My parents said it's okay for me to come to college in California, especially since Charlie's here. They met him a few months ago, and everyone got along great."

"What's not to like about Charlie? Did Tina behave herself?"

"She and my mom got along great." She rolled her eyes. "I think they're already plotting out ways to ruin my life."

"I hope so. Someone's gotta rein you in, and it's not going to be Charlie."

"Mom said it would be good if you're in California, too." She slid a glance toward Dylan talking with the other men. "You are moving out here for good, aren't you?"

"I am, right back to Coral Cove."

The other women had wandered back to their men—good men, strong men—men who took care of their families and the people they loved, men who took pride in their communities.

Dylan ambled toward her and cupped her face

in his capable hands. "Why that half smile on your lips?"

"I was comparing you men. You're all alike, you know."

"Uh-oh. When a woman starts saying things like *men are all alike,* it might be time to break out the flowers and chocolate."

She punched him in the arm because, well, she'd always punched him in the arm. "It's not a bad thing. I was just noticing how protective you all are, how you all saved the day here in town in your own ways."

"Yeah, we're the guardians of Coral Cove."

"You're right. You are." She entwined her arms around Dylan's neck and he planted a kiss on her lips. She'd finally found her own guardian, a guardian of Coral Cove…and a guardian of her heart.

* * * * *

LARGER-PRINT BOOKS!
GET 2 FREE LARGER-PRINT NOVELS PLUS
2 FREE GIFTS!

⬥™ Harlequin®

INTRIGUE®

BREATHTAKING ROMANTIC SUSPENSE

YES! Please send me 2 FREE LARGER-PRINT Harlequin Intrigue® novels and my 2 FREE gifts (gifts are worth about $10). After receiving them, if I don't wish to receive any more books, I can return the shipping statement marked "cancel." If I don't cancel, I will receive 6 brand-new novels every month and be billed just $5.24 per book in the U.S. or $5.99 per book in Canada. That's a saving of at least 13% off the cover price! It's quite a bargain! Shipping and handling is just 50¢ per book in the U.S. and 75¢ per book in Canada.* I understand that accepting the 2 free books and gifts places me under no obligation to buy anything. I can always return a shipment and cancel at any time. Even if I never buy another book, the two free books and gifts are mine to keep forever.

199/399 HDN FERE

Name _____ (PLEASE PRINT) _____

Address _____ Apt. # _____

City _____ State/Prov. _____ Zip/Postal Code _____

Signature (if under 18, a parent or guardian must sign) _____

Mail to the **Reader Service:**
IN U.S.A.: P.O. Box 1867, Buffalo, NY 14240-1867
IN CANADA: P.O. Box 609, Fort Erie, Ontario L2A 5X3

Not valid for current subscribers to Harlequin Intrigue Larger-Print books.

**Are you a subscriber to Harlequin Intrigue books
and want to receive the larger-print edition?
Call 1-800-873-8635 today or visit www.ReaderService.com.**

* Terms and prices subject to change without notice. Prices do not include applicable taxes. Sales tax applicable in N.Y. Canadian residents will be charged applicable taxes. Offer not valid in Quebec. This offer is limited to one order per household. All orders subject to credit approval. Credit or debit balances in a customer's account(s) may be offset by any other outstanding balance owed by or to the customer. Please allow 4 to 6 weeks for delivery. Offer available while quantities last.

Your Privacy—The Reader Service is committed to protecting your privacy. Our Privacy Policy is available online at www.ReaderService.com or upon request from the Reader Service.

We make a portion of our mailing list available to reputable third parties that offer products we believe may interest you. If you prefer that we not exchange your name with third parties, or if you wish to clarify or modify your communication preferences, please visit us at www.ReaderService.com/consumerchoice or write to us at Reader Service Preference Service, P.O. Box 9062, Buffalo, NY 14269. Include your complete name and address.

HILP11B

The series you love are now available in

LARGER PRINT!

The books are complete and unabridged—
printed in a larger type size to make it
easier on your eyes.

Harlequin
Romance

From the Heart, For the Heart

Harlequin
INTRIGUE
BREATHTAKING ROMANTIC SUSPENSE

Harlequin
Presents

Seduction and Passion Guaranteed!

Harlequin
Super Romance

Exciting, emotional, unexpected!

Try **LARGER PRINT** today!

Visit: www.ReaderService.com
Call: 1-800-873-8635

Harlequin

A *Romance* FOR EVERY MOOD™

www.ReaderService.com

HLPDIR11

FAMOUS FAMILIES

YES! Please send me the *Famous Families* collection featuring the Fortunes, the Bravos, the McCabes and the Cavanaughs. This collection will begin with 3 FREE BOOKS and 2 FREE GIFTS in my very first shipment— and more valuable free gifts will follow! My books will arrive in 8 monthly shipments until I have the entire 51-book *Famous Families* collection. I will receive 2-3 free books in each shipment and I will pay just $4.49 U.S./$5.39 CDN for each of the other 4 books in each shipment, plus $2.99 for shipping and handling.* If I decide to keep the entire collection, I'll only have paid for 32 books because 19 books are free. I understand that accepting the 3 free books and gifts places me under no obligation to buy anything. I can always return a shipment and cancel at any time. My free books and gifts are mine to keep no matter what I decide.

268 HCN 0387   468 HCN 0387

Name _____ (PLEASE PRINT)

Address _____ Apt. #

City _____ State/Prov. _____ Zip/Postal Code

Signature (if under 18, a parent or guardian must sign)

Mail to the **Reader Service**:
IN U.S.A.: P.O. Box 1867, Buffalo, NY 14240-1867
IN CANADA: P.O. Box 609, Fort Erie, Ontario L2A 5X3

* Terms and prices subject to change without notice. Prices do not include applicable taxes. Sales tax applicable in N.Y. Canadian residents will be charged applicable taxes. This offer is limited to one order per household. All orders subject to approval. Credit or debit balances in a customer's account(s) may be offset by any other outstanding balance owed by or to the customer. Please allow 4 to 6 weeks for delivery. Offer available while quantities last. Offer not available to Quebec residents.

Your Privacy— The Reader Service is committed to protecting your privacy. Our Privacy Policy is available online at www.ReaderService.com or upon request from the Reader Service.
We make a portion of our mailing list available to reputable third parties that offer products we believe may interest you. If you prefer that we not exchange your name with third parties, or if you wish to clarify or modify your communication preferences, please visit us at www.ReaderService.com/consumerschoice or write to us at Reader Service Preference Service, P.O. Box 9062, Buffalo, NY 14269. Include your complete name and address.

FFBPA12

ReaderService.com

Manage your account online!

- Review your order history
- Manage your payments
- Update your address

*We've designed
the Reader Service website
just for you.*

Enjoy all the features!

- Reader excerpts from any series
- Respond to mailings and
  special monthly offers
- Discover new series available to you
- Browse the Bonus Bucks catalogue
- Share your feedback

Visit us at:
ReaderService.com

RS12